# Seaglass

## Selected Entries from the Black Pear Press Short Story Competition 2014

Edited by Black Pear Press

With contributions by the entrants in the 2014
Black Pear Press Short Story Competition

Thanks and acknowledgements to Judges:
Alison May
Rod Griffiths
Tony Judge

**Black Pear Press**

**Seaglass And Other Stories**

First published in December 2014 by Black Pear Press
www.blackpear.net

Copyright © Contributors 2014

All rights reserved.

Compiled & edited by:
Black Pear Press

No part of this publication may be reproduced, copied, stored
in a retrieval system, or transmitted in any form or by any means
without prior permission in writing from the copyright holder. Nor
may it be otherwise circulated in any form or binding or cover other
than the one in which it is published and without conditions
including this condition being imposed on subsequent purchasers.

All the characters in this publication, other than those clearly in
the public domain, are fictitious and any resemblance to real
persons, living or dead, is purely coincidental.

ISBN: 978-1-910322-14-7

Cover design by Black Pear Press
from glasswork by Lois Parker

# Competition Winners

**First prize:**
Rebecca Burns – *Seaglass*

**Runner-up:**
Pam Plumb – *Sleeping Dragons*

**Shortlisted entries:**
Kevin Brooke – *The Jogger In The Park*
Rebecca Burns – *Seaglass*
Jackie Buxton – *Fly Joe!*
Joanne Derrick – *Liar! Liar! Pants On Fire!*
Richard Anthony Dunford – *Pseudonym*
Graeme Hall – *The Faraday Cage*
Meganne Hearne – *A New Life*
Diane Simmons – *Stopping In*
Pam Plumb – *Sleeping Dragons*
Alison Wassell – *No Cause For Concern*

Congratulations to our prizewinners!

The judges said that *Seaglass* stood out for the writer Rebecca Burns' ability to show rather than tell the story. This short story evokes a glassmaker's life through a few well-written scenes.

The judges were captivated by the characterisation and setting of runner-up Pam Plumb's story *Sleeping Dragons*.

Judge and award-winning writer Alison May said, 'In general the standard of the shortlisted stories was good. I was impressed with the range of stories and styles. The most successful stories were those which evoked a strong sense of character and situation, bearing out the well-worn adage that writers should "show, not tell".'

# Introduction

A short story is a window onto a different world. The reader gets to gaze upon that imaginary universe, but their time there is brief. The challenge for the writer is to make that brief glimpse as evocative as possible, to cram those few transitory moments full of character and emotion, so that the story satisfies but also tempts the reader back to look again.

Short stories are more than simply cut down versions of their longer cousins, the novels. They are the single pop of flavour from a perfect piece of chocolate, compared to the drawn-out feast of a three-course meal. A short story can squeeze its way into the snatched me-time moments of a reader's life, and transport their mind and soul to a different place.

The places created by the writers included in this anthology are as diverse as they are enticing. You'll be invited to share the quandary of a man preparing to leave his homeland. You'll sit alongside a grandfather caring for a wide-eyed child. You'll be transported into the messed up mind of a struggling artist, and pick up weathered pebbles of glass from the shoreline, each piece telling a story of its own. Each new story offers a new world and a new set of lives twisting their way through time.

It was a privilege for me to read all of the shortlisted stories, now included in *Seaglass and Other Stories*. I hope you enjoy this full collection just as much.

Alison May
November 2014

# Contents

Competition Winners ............................................................. iii

Introduction ........................................................................ iv

Contents ............................................................................... v

More Anthologies from Black Pear Press ........................... vi

Seaglass – Rebecca Burns ..................................................... 1

Sleeping Dragons – Pam Plumb ............................................ 6

A New Life – Meganne Hearne ........................................... 10

As A Moat Defensive To A House – Brian Comber ........ 15

Fly Joe! – Jackie Buxton ....................................................... 19

I Have Put Away Childish Things – Brian Comber .......... 24

Liar, Liar! Pants On Fire! – Joanne Derrick ...................... 29

Meteors – Jade Chen ............................................................ 32

No Cause For Concern – Alison Wassell ............................ 36

Pseudonym – Richard Anthony Dunford .......................... 41

Starry, Starry Night – Meganne Hearne ............................ 46

Stopping In – Diane Simmons ............................................. 49

The Art Expert's Child – Jenifer Granger ......................... 54

The Expediter – James Starke .............................................. 59

The Faraday Cage – Graeme Hall ........................................ 64

The Jogger In The Park – Kevin Brooke ............................ 68

The Missus – Sue Thomas .................................................... 72

The Price Of Love – Joseph Govan ..................................... 75

The Snip – Claudia Crutwell ................................................ 79

Unfinished Business – Courtney Jennings .......................... 84

# More Anthologies from Black Pear Press

## Short Stories:
*Short Stories from Black Pear - Volume 1*
A collection of short stories from various Worcestershire-based authors including humour, true life, science fiction, horror and some almost impossible to categorise.
Paperback ISBN:     978-0-9927755-0-6
eBook ISBN:         978-0-9927755-2-0

## Flash Fiction:
*Flashes of Fiction 2013*
Winners and selected entries from the Worcestershire LitFest & Fringe Flash Fiction Competition 2013. Write a short story in under 300 words—73 different stories in one book.
Paperback ISBN:     978-0-9927755-1-3
eBook ISBN:         978-0-9927755-3-7

*Fifty Flashes of Fiction*
Winners and selected entries from the Worcestershire LitFest & Fringe Flash Fiction Competition 2014.
Paperback ISBN:     978-1-910322-10-9
eBook ISBN:         978-1-910322-11-6

## Young Writers - Aged 7 - 17
*Worcestershire Young Writers Competition Anthology 2014*
Read the early work of budding fiction writers: Winners and selected entries from the Worcestershire Young Writers Competition 2014.
Paperback ISBN:     978-1-910322-12-3
eBook ISBN:         978-1-910322-13-0

www.blackpear.net

# Seaglass – Rebecca Burns

*Young piece. About half an inch in diameter, though typically oval shaped. Green, smearing of brown on one edge. Frosted. No apparent nicks on the surface. Found on Seaham Beach at low tide. Common colour, easy to pair; earring set. Potential value in gift/craft shop market.*

A way in, if you could stick the heat. Glassmaking was devilish work; sometimes Billy wondered if he'd turn and find the man by his side, stripped to the waist alike, was Lucifer himself. The walls of the furnace peeled with fire; bricks were replaced every half year or more, blackened on one side. Men poured batch into the mould and then retreated, letting the flames do its work.

'You're a runner, so run,' and Billy would be dispatched to the Hare and Hounds for beer. The men drank while they worked, never caring that Billy had passed over his grandfather's pocket-watch to the barman, and that he hoped to reclaim it when the men paid up. Running for beer was a way in, a sliding dance into a job. They called him Mooney, on account of his round face.

The glass works belched smoke onto the shoreline day and night. The workers, wedged tight into their little houses, heard the crackle of chimneys, like stars falling.

'Shut that fecking window!' and Billy's mam would slam the glass shut. 'I hate the smell worse than the gulls.'

Smoke pressed down on the town, folding over the edges of the sea, so that water would sometimes catch a man leaving the works at the dead of night. The day shift would find him, washed up on the pebbles. Sometimes not.

Then Billy saw his first man burnt and kept his stomach. Not for Billy the loss of his breakfast, even when the poor soul was carried past him. The man's chest, from his throat to his melted belt, had bubbled up like belly pork. Older men turned away. Hands strayed to shining scars on their own bodies. But not Billy. Mooney showed spit, it was observed. He collected his grandfather's pocket-watch from the Hare and Hounds and started taking the waste bits down to the sea.

'Still at their beck and call,' his mam sneered and refused to call him Mooney, though his brothers did. He didn't mind carrying the wooden crates of glass down to the shoreline and throwing the pieces in. He could swing his arms out and watch shards fall in a cloud. Or he could skim them, stone-like, over the surface. A slice of green, a slice of brown. Glass that had shattered in the furnace and not stood up to the test. He watched the sea swallow it whole.

*Edges worn away. Amber colour, irregular shape but workable. About an inch long. Chip on one side, can be hidden by clasp. Suitable for a pendant.*

The baby had colic, the shouty kind that made Billy's teeth ache. Walls were thin; Isobel's screams lapped into his sleep. Esme saw to her, trying to persuade their squalling daughter to lick down a tonic.

The hours between home and work blurred together so that, sometimes, Billy would snap into himself and realise he was not standing by the stove, heating milk, but was beside his men, overseeing the building of crates for carrying bottles, his mouth open but only empty, tired air flowing out. The baby sucked the life from him and Esme both; the sight of his wife's breasts after feeding shocked him. When he was especially tired, he hated Isobel.

'Won't always be this way, Mooney.' Esme's cool voice as she fell in beside him after getting up once more in the night. 'She'll sleep through soon, you'll see.' Her knees and elbows knocked into him and made Billy think of a pelican, the kind he sometimes saw in the early morning on the shoreline. When she lay on him and her hair fell down, he thought of seaweed.

Medicine bottles were packed down with straw and lids nailed onto the crates. The glass was an odd, yellow colour. He took a rejected bottle home to Esme, setting it on the table with flowers. She was delighted. 'The colour is all the fashion now.' When the flowers died, she washed it out and put it on the windowsill, so the sun caught it as it moved around their little house. Isobel broke it, tipping it onto the stone floor with flailing arms, and Esme cried. She gathered up all the pieces and took them down to the shore herself and threw them into the water.

*Light blue. A fault throughout, but not enough for it to fracture. Adds to the appeal. Large piece, almost two inches in length. Weathered on the edges. Potential value on online market.*

They stopped loving each other before Isobel turned five; Esme had caught him swinging for the child with a poker and that had been the start of it. But she'd stopped calling him Mooney sometime before. Even started calling him William when he took up the overseeing of furnace building. He told his mam the extra money went to her head.

Of course they would not separate, so he moved Isobel out of her room and in with her mother, and slept in his daughter's narrow cot. He didn't mind, actually, preferring the tight way the bedframe gripped his body. It was like being a child again, crushed up against his brothers.

There was money in cutting bricks for the furnace, but it was thankless work. His men hacked out huge blocks from the stones brought over from the Middlesborough quarries, replacing burned bricks that lined the seat of the terrible fires. They worked the furnaces in a circle, every month pulling out dead stone, moving onto the next furnace a month later. All the time, heat from the not-quite-dead coals swelled their faces.

Blue batch for ink bottles, bright lime for jars of pickled fruit: the glass works was expanding. Beer bottles still gave them the most work, but even that felt tired to Billy. Now he sat with the bosses at dinner-time. He listened out for talk about new techniques, new ways of firing glass. He listened to tales of bottles being shipped to Africa, India, to strange lands so far away they might as well have been the moon. The boss told a tale of his brother, fighting the

Boers, receiving treatment in some dusty station, and how the man cried over a blue bottle of salts used to clean wounds. 'Recognised the mark, didn't he, of this factory,' and Billy was amazed to see that men of money could cry just the same as him.

*Rare purple. Frosted as usual, but colour is deep. Inch in length, quite thick and heavy. High resale value, especially if turned into a brooch or clasp.*

His new wife was scandalous when she ate and Billy couldn't stop watching. Clarissa spoke with her mouth full, licked her fingers. She sucked chicken bones dry. She picked off fat and gristle. She snored and threw out her arms in her sleep, once knocking Billy from their bed. When Isobel visited, she squeezed the girl to her chest; she held Billy tightly in place when he climbed on top, nightly, only letting him go when she was content.

He thought he had gone mad but was powerless. Clarissa thundered about his house, hips barrelling side to side. She barged aside any trace of long-dead Esme, though not in an unkind way. She just did not understand what it meant to tread carefully, to be quiet. Once, one Christmas when they stayed overnight at the Boss's house, Billy had to stuff the corner of a bed sheet in her mouth and roll off her in a hurry.

The men sniggered, he knew, but he tried to ignore it, gliding through the works as though he had not a care. For two horrible weeks, Clarissa took up packing purple syrup bottles in crates, complaining she could not know what it was like for the wives they gave money to, without doing the work herself. The women gawped at her, sucking their teeth when she broke bottles with her fat hands.

There were other storms, which appeared each month. He knew when their maid dragged the large tin bucket into the garden and soaked Clarissa's underwear that there would be weeping again. She was too big for babies, she said. Her belly, pushed against his back when they lay together, was as hard as rock. He could not imagine a child living in there. But then the surge of tears would stop and it would be calm again; Clarissa would bake and Billy would go to the works, where orders had swelled again, broken glass was taken down to the sea, and rich housewives in Chelsea waited for their coloured vases from the natives up north.

# Sleeping Dragons – Pam Plumb

'How will we know?' says Sophie, her face a scrunch of concentration.

He turns to look at the glass bowl. Reflections from the dark wood table soil the water. 'You'll nah.' He rolls his tongue around his mouth as if checking his teeth are in. 'They'll grow legs at the back first.'

Sophie looks at him, searching the deep grooved criss-crosses of his face.

'How long does it take? Will I still be here?'

'Aye, lass. Nay bother.' His wink is faster than a blink but Sophie doesn't miss it. She smiles and turns back to watch the fat-bodied tadpoles in the bowl and wonders why they don't bump into each other.

'Do you think they miss their mum?' she says.

He rubs the side of his nose. 'Nay, lass. They've never known her.' He walks through to the kitchen and Sophie hears him set the kettle on the hob.

She looks at her hands, remembering how the frogspawn slimed through her fingers into the jar. Now her palms are dry, her fingers unwebbed by any gloop. Dirt, black as the fat darting bodies, hunkers in the grooves of her skin and flecks her fingernails. She rubs her hands on her jeans and walks to the kitchen, her toes curling on the cold slate floor.

'What's for breakfast, Granddad?'

'You've been here a week. You should nah, it's 'Grandda' or there's nay breakfast.'

Despite his frown Sophie sees a half smile get ready to unfurl itself from the crease around his mouth. She skips across the floor and hugs his arm. Ancient pipe smoke drifts out from the thick green twine of his jacket.

'Mum says I have to call you 'Granddad'.'

He peels her fingers away and moves over to the fridge. 'Aye, well, your mam…' He shakes his head and pulls out a side of bacon and slams it down. 'Now. Do you want eggs and bacon or bacon and eggs?'

Sophie pretends to think, her finger pressed to her forehead. Then she forgets herself and jumps and claps and shouts, 'Bacon and eggs, bacon and eggs.'

His smile breaks full sail.

Today clouds like sleeping dragons guard the sky, keeping the sun at bay. Sophie watches the soil tumble back into the groove that he's just made. He draws his trowel along the line again then stands and nods.

Out of the crease of her hand Sophie nips at the seeds and smidges them along the shallow furrow. Black and round, like magic beans, they disappear into the soil.

'What now, Grandda?'

'Cover them over. Just a little.'

'Then can I water them?' She watches him, sees his mouth twitch.

The awful ring of the telephone from the house tightens his face, reels in his smile. He tries a wink but it is slow and heavy. Turning back to the house he drops the trowel. It lies entrenched up to its handle.

Sophie hears him talking. His words are pecked at by the blackbirds, but she can still hear his low burr. She picks up the watering can. A two-handed job to water the seeds. His deep voice is drowned out by the splashing. A worm gets caught in the shower. Stripped of its mud coat Sophie sees its insides squirm. As it finds secret slices of emptiness in the earth she wonders if it is a mummy or a daddy worm. Or even a lost baby worm.

The slam of the back door makes her back stiffen. She waits, watches the worm's journey until she hears him beside her, rubbing his face, the bristles crackling against his palm. He smells angry, his pipe lit and blowing out puffs of dragon smoke. 'Your mam. Saturday afternoon.'

Sophie picks up the trowel and pushes it into his free hand.

'Can we do the carrots now?'

She watches him. Sees one watery wink.

He pats his jacket pockets and pulls out the seeds. 'Aye, lass. Nay bother.'

After her bath she grabs Pink Rabbit and gets into bed. Her hot skin is plucked by the chill air trapped under the covers and she giggles a shiver. The sheets smell green, smell of the cold, of the outside.

'Settle down or we'll have nay time.'

She wants to ask him about the tadpoles. No legs today. She knows she will miss them growing up. She watches him rub his nose and sniff. She wonders if he can smell her. She hopes she smells of ice cream and new shoes. He always smells of dragon smoke and mud. 'Will we finish the story tonight?'

'Aye, nay bother.' Then he winks and turns the page though he knows the words by heart.

Only two pages on and Sophie hears his low burr begin to knit the words together. Woven into each breath they float down and tuck themselves in around her. Her eyes close before he turns out the light.

The last orange slice of the sun makes Sophie cover her eyes as she watches the car come down the track. Murky blasts of dirt billow up behind its wheels.

'Come here, lass.'

She turns to see him at the door, half looking at her and half looking at the car. 'Come and look at the tadpoles.'

Sophie glances back at the car then skips across the yard. Inside, the evening light has settled in. He switches on the table lamp. Sophie gets close up to the bowl, her breath smudging the glass. Two of the tadpoles have legs. The others are a day behind, fatter now but still smooth like bullets.

The car door slams and Sophie hears a man and a woman talking.

'Will you keep them for me? I might be back,' says Sophie.

She watches him. The creases of his face turn themselves into a smile. He rubs the side of his nose. The skin on his finger is lined with trams of grime that might be years old.

'Aye, lass. Nay bother.'

# A New Life – Meganne Hearne

Conor sighed, his large tanned hands holding his head. Fiona would be in the front room, fastening the belt around her best dress, the one he had bought when they were still courting two years ago; putting on her white cotton gloves. Those bloody gloves. It wasn't right that she should have to cover her work-worn hands. This was not the life he had promised when he had proposed at the end of the war.

Squeezing the bridge of his nose he tried to push away the images of how they now struggled to survive in Dublin. When they realised his wage wasn't enough, Fiona had insisted Conor let her take in laundry to make up the shortfall.

Fiona had gone to her friends and neighbours, speaking only to the women. She would not have Conor's reputation damaged in any way. She had filled her days with laundry and mending, supplementing enough for them to meet their needs and for Conor to have a weekly drink with Fiona's brother—and Conor's lifelong friend— Sean and for the occasional small luxury. The first of these had been Fiona's cotton gloves, and Conor had despised them immediately.

Conor had not told Fiona about Sean's plans. There was a ship leaving later that night offering cheap passage to Australia and the promise of a better life. Sean would be on it, no matter what. He had tried to persuade Conor to join him, had even bought a spare ticket to reserve his place.

'Fiona'll be fine,' he had insisted when Conor had objected. 'The family will see that she's looked after, and as soon as you've got something sorted out, you can send for her. They're just giving it away out there.' He was insistent, his enthusiasm contagious, and Conor had desperately wanted to say yes. He had heard the stories, seen the posters. Many had gone already, their infrequent letters painting vibrant pictures.

Conor had stared at his beer and thought about Fiona's hands, how she had worked just as hard as he, and always put food on the table and kept house.

His father constantly pestered him, when was he going to give him his first grandchild? Conor didn't have the heart to tell him both he and Fiona were too exhausted most of the time to do anything other than sleep. He knew Fiona's mother often raised the same question, though with greater criticism of Fiona. Fiona would always reply that when God wanted her to give Conor a child, God would make it so.

Back in the present, Conor tried to cheer up. Tonight's cinema visit was a rare treat, Fiona deserved better than to share it with a misery. Perhaps it was just the thought of losing Sean. Or maybe it was knowing that Sean had the guts to improve his future while he, Conor, stayed at home and struggled all his life, as had countless generations before.

Conor moved to watch his wife. He admired her strength and stamina, the way she always acted with pride and dignity. Fiona saw his reflection and turned, flashing him a smile. She gave him a twirl and raised herself on tiptoes to plant a kiss on his lips, cupping his face with her hands. Her piercing blue eyes held his as he wrapped his arms around her.

'You're beautiful.' Conor saw Fiona as if for the first time: her strong features, the mass of dark hair she held in check under her bonnet.

'Why, thank you, you're not so bad yourself.' She teased him with another kiss then grabbed his hand and danced past him. 'Come on, we'll be late.'

Walking to the cinema, they passed many people heading towards the docks. Among them was Sean. Seeing them, he ran over and clapped Conor on the back. He seized Fiona in a tight embrace.

'Fiona, I love you and you'll always be my little sis. Remember that.'

'What's the matter, Sean, what's wrong?'

'Wrong? Nothing, couldn't be better in fact.' Fiona smiled. Sean was always full of nervous energy, unable to keep still for a moment. 'Do us a favour would you, Fiona? Check in on Ma and Da tomorrow? Will you do that for me?' Fiona nodded.

'Are you sure there's nothing wrong, Sean?'

'No, pet, nothing wrong, but promise me you'll do that?'

'Okay, I promise, I'll call in on them tomorrow.'

'Excellent, good girl. Right, just give me a moment with this husband of yours, would you?' He hugged Fiona tight with his powerful arms and planted a kiss by her ear. Fiona laughed as he let her go.

'One minute, I'm not going to miss the feature on your account!' She wandered over to the shops to give the men space.

'I've got your ticket right here.' Sean pulled two tickets from his pocket. 'You have to come, you know it makes sense. A little bit of time and effort is all it needs, then you can send for Fiona to join you. Go on, Conor, say you'll come.' Conor sighed. It was extremely tempting. Had he been single, he would not have thought twice.

'Don't, Sean, please.' He shook his head. 'I can't see Fiona hurt. It's bad enough she'll be losing you.'

'But if we both go, she can join us in a couple of months. It'll be fantastic, the chance of a lifetime. What do you say?' Conor sighed and looked at Fiona, admiring the dresses in Milligan's shop window that were beyond his means to give her. Unable to speak, he shook his head again. 'Okay, here's the deal. I'll wait in that pub for one hour. The ship sails at midnight and last boarding is at ten.' He clapped Conor on the shoulder. 'You're a good man, Conor, you've been a good mate to me all these years. I'll see you soon.' Sean walked confidently into the bar. Conor watched, torn.

Fiona returned and took Conor's hand.

'Everything okay?'

'Why shouldn't it be?' Conor's tone was sharper than he had intended. 'I'm sorry, come on, we'd better shift.' Fiona squeezed his hand.

At the cinema, Conor collected the tickets and they took their seats just as the lights went down. Fiona snuggled into him as the short film began, the prelude to the main feature.

Conor didn't take any of the film in. His mind was on Sean and the spare ticket. He silently ran through the arguments against his going, but now they sounded weak. He knew that if he didn't go now, with Sean, he would never raise the courage again. It was such a fantastic opportunity, you couldn't lose out there. And it wouldn't be long before Fiona could come out and join him, and she need never work—or wear those bloody gloves—again.

Patting Fiona's hand, Conor whispered in her ear that he was going to get a drink. He walked briskly out of the foyer and down the street to where Sean had waited. How much time had passed? Although he was convinced he was doing the right thing, a small part of Conor hoped that Sean—and the spare ticket—would have already left. No doubt Sean would be able to sell it for a profit on the docks; there were always more people wanting passage than the ship could accommodate.

Sean stood just outside the doorway, pulling his jacket on, a cigarette dangling from his lip. His duffel bag propped against the wall, he had watched the minutes tick by on the clock in the square. When half past nine came and Sean still hadn't shown up, he had been disappointed but glad there would be an extra person around to support Fiona and his parents.

Swinging the bag onto his shoulder, he started towards the docks.

'Sean!' The call stopped him and he swung round, saw Conor breaking into a run to catch up with him.

'Conor. Good man, best get a move on.' They walked briskly, milling with the others waiting to board and those still hoping to get a ticket.

'I've no bag,' Conor warned.

'I packed double. I knew you'd come.' It had always been like this; Sean leading, Conor anxious not to miss out on any of the excitement. He hoped he was doing the right thing. He didn't dare think too much about Fiona right now. He was doing this for her, for their future and the new life ahead of them. He just hoped she would forgive him.

In the cinema, Fiona rubbed her hand tenderly over her belly. Conor had seemed rather distracted tonight; perhaps he had guessed her news already. She hoped he wouldn't be too angry; they had wanted to wait a bit longer until they had a little more money, but God had chosen to bless them now. Please let him be happy, she prayed as the feature started, the seat next to her still empty.

# As A Moat Defensive To A House – Brian Comber

Always a dark suit for a funeral; I got that silver-backed brush to get rid of the fibres and as I brush they float and are caught in the harsh winter morning light. A sober tie, you see some that have got no class with bright colours for a tie and modern stuff about celebrating a life, but I don't get it. A funeral is for mourning. I got no medals but if you have, it's a chance to show 'em, Bill'll have 'em.

They asked me about music and I suggested 'A Whiter Shade of Pale' as I know that always gets them going. You want something to make 'em think and something to make 'em cry.

He was a good old boy really and he's known round these parts, there'll be a good turnout and a full pub after.

He started off doing errands round the docks and making himself useful. He always walked that line, on the edges of trouble but he always melted away when there was a reckoning. People can respect that, people liked Tommy, he was lucky and people like being with lucky men; they hope it rubs off.

Cuff links, my dad's, he said he got them from a German. Tortoiseshell with little cracks and I hold 'em up to the light and I think of the creature that it once was and hot countries where I've never been. They're the only set I've got but you only need the one.

A morning funeral is more respectful on account of the drinking, but these days it don't seem to make a difference when you have it, The Crown used to be the place but not now as its sold on. In the old days you could rely on people holding their drink, but not now, we don't want a scene. I'll put a bit behind the bar.

Tommy helped me in the seventies when the docks went and there was no work; he built up that firm, played a long game, argued hard in upstairs rooms and stuffed a roll in my pocket when no one was looking, more than once, so we could have a Christmas.

There's been a lot of changes, people don't talk as much, always on the phone or the web; I can't see the point of that; if you want to talk, you get a pint and have it out in a corner of the public bar; that's where I get business done and that's where I heard what he'd done. There are things you don't do, even nowadays when no one seems to know right from wrong; there are standards; without rules we're just like that pack of Rotherhithe dogs that no one can catch.

You think you know a man: I've seen Tommy quieten a bar room with a stare, seen him sob like a baby and squeal like a pig, seen him getting in the back of Rollers without a look back and just a flick of a ciggie. I've clasped his hand in his triumphs and I was the one who put my arm round his shoulders when he came out of court as a twenty year old, a cigarette paper from going down.

I've looked into those yellowed eyes and seen a school mate staring back, one who didn't grass me up when he could've done when we burned that shop. And I thought I knew the man.

But there are wheels within wheels and depths of the heart, I don't know. I thought I knew the man.

You don't forget where you're from or who you are but there's plenty who try. Tommy put his boy through private school; he said he didn't want him mixing with the likes of me. But last I heard his son's in the Gulf with his American missus and he never comes to visit, not even when Peg was in the hospital. Can't call that gratitude. He probably saw something he didn't like in his old dad and put as many miles between them as he could. Trying to escape the smell of the river and the shame at school when the stories came out.

Me and Tommy spent a lot of our life sticking together, defending our turf and looking after our own. People used to ask me what he was planning. I used to say, 'Ask him yourself,' but they never did, they were too scared of him, but not so much of me, like I was his kid brother, but there's only a fortnight between us.

Which is why I don't rightly understand what he did, can't make head nor tail.

There was a programme on the telly the other night about a tribe somewhere and they had all these rituals and ceremonies, ways of dealing with life and death. When someone died they all knew what to do, when someone got married, they all did what they did since Adam was a lad; they knew the rules and no one thought any different, that's how it seemed to me. And if someone did break the rules of the tribe they had to leave, walk out into the forest and not come back. The programme didn't say whether this still happens but I think in the old days it meant an early end, eaten by a jaguar or strung up by another tribe, but mostly it was the shame rather than the fear that kept the tribe together. They didn't have many rules and we've got thousands, but the point is the same: not against your own tribe, not your own tribe, Tommy.

We both helped old Arthur when he couldn't stand and couldn't hold it in, we both went round because he wouldn't let no one else through the door, but I tailed off and Tommy kept going until near the end. He said to me, you've got to look after the old 'uns, what are you when you've lost face? He took his hand the last time he made it to the Crown and the pub went still as we all knew that was his last pint; Tommy held his hand, tender like, until he'd finished and quietly took him home. We all drank to him when the doors swung closed.

So he knew about old age and all the traps, which makes what he did so difficult to fathom.

But that's the thing, you can't understand. There's dirt and business and we all know about that and there's cruelty and things you wouldn't do to a dog.

Tommy was a good man: his turning a blind eye at the yard, his dealing with bailiffs and his paying respects and holding the line. With his community spirit and man of the people, he made his mark, but you don't piss inside your own tent. Me and Tom learned right from wrong at Sunday school; I always followed what was said and got the fear in me for what God might do to me if I did wrong, but Tommy never could follow a lesson. Old Kendrick was always shouting at him and standing him in the corner. He couldn't settle to learning, he was always looking out across the tarmac to the allotments and beyond. The church will tell you what's what, but you got to work it out for yourself, the rules you play by when you lay your head down at night. I've not slept for years but I know Tommy sleeps well; when he kipped on my floor he slept like a baby, I walked round him. You only sleep like that when you've got no worries. Or no conscience. Or no soul.

There'll be a good show and one or two widows with knowing nods to each other and a secret smile.

Now for the hard part. Can't put this off now, the car'll be here soon.

I'm off to see Tommy with the Polish lad who's a bit handy. We'll be letting Tommy know what we're planning Thursday week.

There'll be a bit of a struggle and some shouting but he'll give up pretty soon, he knows the rules. I just hope he keeps his dignity; we've all got to go sometime, Tommy, and you left us no choice.

I've seen men die and I can cope with looking but the sounds stay with you, I can't stand anyone begging, we've got to make it quick. We've checked for cameras, we've all got hats and no one's talking.

It's like the London clay or Marble Arch, solid and immovable, the laws that govern us, the ties that bind, given out at birth, like the colour of your eyes.

You have to do the right thing, because how can we carry on if you don't? That's just the way it is.

Last look in the mirror, not bad, not bad at all, now I can hear a car pulling up.

Right-ho, Tommy boy, let's go and shake hands, one last time.

# Fly Joe! – Jackie Buxton

Hesta placed the food on the table in front of him, took the napkin and shook it to reveal a worn square.

'I've brought you lamb with redcurrant sauce and dumplings,' she said, tucking the napkin into his collar. 'Well, strictly it's not lamb but a couple of pieces of rubber from the bottom of me boots. I gave them a quick spruce up with the hose before of course, although being in the chicken pen, some of the poo does get a bit squashed in the grooves. We didn't have as many redcurrants as I'd have liked—been too hot, surprisingly—so I had to take the ones from near the ground; the ones you tell me not to touch because the fox might have pee'd on 'em. And the dumplings? Well, they're just dumplings, like me mum used to make, the very finest with snips of bacon. But you were never too keen on dumplings, were you? Anyway, there we are, shall I feed you now?' she asked, finally sitting down on the edge of the bed and picking up the spoon.

Joe would have smiled if he could. Instead, he raised an eyebrow.

'This stomach was expensive,' his T-shirt shouted through thick white lettering buffering up to the mound of his stomach. Her eyes lingered on the hillock; a perfect sphere. Ever since this beanpole of a husband had been introduced to steroids and constipation, he'd stuffed a bowling ball underneath his clothes.

She whispered again, 'Shall I feed you?'

Joe blinked once for no and then several times in rapid succession.

'Okay,' Hesta said, jumping from the edge of the bed and snatching the napkin from his neck and the plate from where his hands should have reached. 'I'll leave you with the snooker.'

Joe blinked twice.

'Day one,' she said, as she darted from the room with his dinner in her hands. She sat herself down at the two-drawer table in the kitchen, and stabbed her fork into the lamb. 'Day one accomplished,' she repeated. How long would it take?

She looked around her kitchen which hadn't been decorated for over nine years and tutted. She took in the poppy-speckled wallpaper, peeling itself from the wall where it met the yellowing tiles around the chipped Belfast sink. She would re-decorate. In fact, she'd do the whole house. It would mark the new start.

The second day Hesta made brown spaghetti with a spicy ratatouille sauce full of onions, burnt to a crisp, just like Joe didn't like them. Really, he was a 'meat and two veg' man. He was a farmer. 'Farmers eat meat, Hest,' he'd said in the early days, smiling at the thought that she could consider serving him anything else. He had a voracious appetite back then, being outside all day, running around the fields rounding up the sheep, 'Braveheart', in particular. Braveheart was the only sheep he'd ever named due to her valiant and most un-sheep-like attempts at darting for freedom.

Once Hesta had removed his untouched meal, she returned with his glass of water. Silently she held the straw up to Joe's lips but today he didn't drink. She removed the water, went into the kitchen and ate his dinner.

'Breakfast TV or a DVD?' Hesta asked cheerily on day three. Joe didn't respond. 'A look outside?' she suggested, and Joe gave two blinks. 'No problem,' she said, adjusting the backrest to raise him up to window height. She looked into his eyes and asked if he'd like to be taken into the garden today. She hoped the answer would be no. The carers had helped her transport him yesterday and they'd been shocked how 'wan' he looked, how his cheekbones appeared to be jutting out, which was astonishing when you considered the amount of steroids he was on. Was he drinking enough? Should they call the doctor? And Hesta had been forced to lie.

Joe blinked once. 'Just the window, then.' She pointed towards the small area of light. 'Raining, I'm afraid.' She wished the sun would shine.

When Hesta took Joe his plate of cod in a creamy dill sauce on day four, his eyes were closed. She placed the plate on the table but didn't wheel it under his chin. Instead, she sat herself on the edge of the bed and leaned over him. She put her ear to his chest. Still breathing.

'Time to eat, Joe,' she said, struggling to speak loudly enough. 'Fish in a congealed, gloopy sauce which would make a good flour and water paste.' She looked at him. His eyes were still closed but his chest was moving even though she could hear the saliva clattering around at the back of his throat. She winced. 'No it wouldn't,' she said, faltering for the first time. 'It's nothing like flour and water paste. It's a proper white sauce, with a thimbleful of white wine.' Still his eyes didn't open. 'It's how you like it,' she whispered.

She pressed her lips to his, held them there, her hands curved around his cheeks.

'Fly, Joe!' she said, pulling away just far enough to speak. 'It's time to find your legs.' She wished him well on his journey. She kissed him again, laid her head on his heart. She felt the tiny beats fade to nothing and held his hand until his spirit had flown.

Then she went into the kitchen, scraped his dinner into the bin and poured a drop of washing up liquid into the bowl. And then she wept. She wept until her tears had melted all the bubbles. Then she wiped her eyes with the tea towel, made a cup of coffee and sat down to write the letter.


*Dear Joe,*

*'Assisted Suicide,' they'll call it, the neighbours, the ones who don't understand. They said they'd see me hang if I ever tried it, once they'd heard talk at the post office. I'm not sure where that came from. I told some I'd help you if you asked for it—it didn't seem shocking to me. Why wouldn't I help you? If being your carer is to help you do what you want because you can't do it; if being your wife is wanting you to be happy; if making our marriage vows to love and honour in sickness and in health is something I believed in right back*

*when we stood together at that alter twenty-three years ago, then yes, of course I would help you be free if that's what you wanted more than anything else in the world.*

*For the record, it wasn't 'assisted' was it, because I never laid a finger on you or gave you any drugs and it wasn't 'suicide' either because you didn't kill yourself.*

*You just didn't fancy what I was cooking.*

*I wish you hadn't gone out that morning chasing after Braveheart, beyond the fields and over the road, like you'd done a thousand times before. But I don't regret that you were paralysed. Is that selfish of me? Maybe. But we got to say our goodbyes and for that, I'm grateful.*

*And now? Well, I'm excited for you, Joe, because you've been let loose and by heck, I hope you can fly again. That's all I ask, really. Fly, Joe, far away from your painful world.*

*Goodbye my love, my friend,*

*Hest xx*


Hesta used a corner of the tablecloth to dab at the smudges in the ink from her tears. She breathed out, used both hands to lift herself from the table and strode into the lounge where his bed swamped the whole space. She switched off the snooker.

'Joe, you've got post,' she said, as she had almost every day since they'd moved the bed downstairs. 'You can read it yourself now.' She placed the page on his upturned hand, kissed him on his forehead and then on his lips.

She studied his face. The pain had gone. The more she stared, the more she thought she saw his first smile for nine years. She looked up at the ceiling; it was more than a smile. It was a beam stretching the width of his face from where he was watching over. His arms were outstretched. He was floating. He reached down and pulled her to him, nuzzled his face into her neck. She took in his smell from before; lime shower gel with a faint hint of sheep poo.

She wrapped her arms around her waist and felt his final squeeze before he let her go.

Hesta looked back at his face, the warmth gone. 'You big soppy arse,' she said, and pressed her lips to his once more. Her tears slid off his face. 'No regrets.'

She walked directly to the table as planned, to the base where she'd checked a little too often that the phone was charging. Her hand on the receiver, she breathed out and smiled. Joe had flown.

# I Have Put Away Childish Things – Brian Comber

Traffic passed along the street below the office, the flow fluctuating on a long rhythm with the changing of the lights. Jennifer picked up the pile of applications and leafed through them, noticing key words and names, the first applicant was due to arrive shortly. She tidied her papers and straightened the chairs. She made herself a coffee, the air was heavy but there were no windows she could open. She usually reckoned on a few no shows and hoped this would be over by twelve.

She decided to do a little more preparation and her eye was caught this time by a familiar name; Danny had shortlisted for her, so this was the first time she had looked in detail.

Her initial thought was maybe this was not the same person, it was not an uncommon surname, but a look at the date of birth made her feel increasingly certain. She scanned through the list of short-term, low-paid jobs, with frequent gaps, that made up a hopeful CV, with some pleasure. The selective phrasing and positive nuancing that a CV aims for, could not disguise a working life of low achievement and unrealised ambition.

Angela, or Angie as everyone called her; her thoughts turned back to a hot summer of misery and school avoidance, when Angie had been a daily presence, a smiling girl, superficially charming and responsive to staff, who, in quiet ways, in back corridors, through whispered taunts, brought her life to a standstill.

Her mouth felt dry and she noticed her hand trembled, she thought of the aftermath, the accusations and Angie's denials and protestations, of summer term ending without anything solved and the long holidays ruined by fear and lethargy. They had holidayed in Cornwall that year and her memories, of a boat trip, of a beach barbecue, of her brother windsurfing, are all tainted with the anxiety and nausea that the thought of a return to school would bring.

The crushing weight on her chest in bed the night before the start of the term, sobbing into her pillow as outside a buddleia thrashed her window in an early September storm.

Now she gathered together the applications and slipped them into a folder, picked up her bag and walked down to the level below, pushing through the swing doors to take some deep breaths and to walk off the tremors in her legs.

The interviews passed, faces came and went, she made notes of answers and Helen from HR gave her guidance and advice, but she moved forward in a fog, images flooding her mind, of echoing passageways, canteen smells, hot breath and high metal-framed windows opening onto an emptying playground.

It was Angie's turn, she had been shown to the ante room and Jennifer decided to make her wait. Only a thin wall separated them now and she was reminded of the time she was made to sit outside the staff room, only to find her incoherent entreaties ignored by a headmaster who only gazed at her with contempt and then having to leave and walk past Angie who had waited at the end of the corridor, not daring to meet her eyes.

Angie was called through and sat cautiously; pushing her hair behind her ears and taking off her glasses, Jennifer waited for a glimmer of recognition, but her expression gave nothing away.

Perhaps, thought Jennifer, although Angie loomed large in her memory, Jennifer was of no importance to her and had subsequently disappeared from her past? Towards the end of the interview as the questions wound down Angie tilted her head to one side, half quizzical, half ironic, a gesture which at school had been a precursor to sarcasm or insult. Jennifer wavered; Angie allowed herself a fleeting smile. Her voice came in waves, as if buffered by distance, the moments tightened as the composure that Jennifer had held together until now, threatened to fragment.

That gesture, she thought, she knows.

Angie left, having had no further questions and Jennifer reflected that she has opened up a fluid space between then and now and she feels balanced on a precipice, holding back the reawakened past. When the decision comes it feels like tossing a coin, throwing her life into the hazard. 'We won't take her on,' she says to Helen, then in a heartbeat, 'We'll take her on.'

She is the best candidate. The woman from HR comments on her people skills and Jennifer laughs.

'We'll take her,' she says again and snaps her bag shut.

That desert of time the empty years after school and the life that took a long time to get going, the heaviness in the heart that comes from adolescent damage, those empty miles of time spring shut and now rest in her hands, this is a chance to tidy the historical trail she thinks. She is tired of pushing the world uphill, tired of the diffidence she has when entering a room, the self-help books, the diets, years of unsuitable boys and her exposed fetishistic tattoo which she now sees as self loathing, not ornament.

The day unfurls and she picks at the threads of her concentration.

She walks to the nearby park, where she knows a bench which is usually fairly clean. The park is nearly empty, late morning, a few mothers with toddlers swaddled against the wind.

She leans back and gazes up; it feels like a time to take stock. This is the point to take charge; there is a need to look forward and to approach things differently this time. She feels on the boundary between childhood and adulthood, between chaos and order.

Above crows mob a gull, the raw cries carrying across the open spaces. Children swirl in a spiralling chasing game, as a lone chid stands on the edge of the laughing group, not knowing how to join in. Shouts come from a nearby street where two people are hurling insults about a parking space. A snarling dog with a muzzle is dragged away by an angry man.

The tide is turning in the Pool of London; the towers of the financial institutions are visible rising from the mist.

The world is in a state of war she observes, by sleight of hand or hand to hand fighting, this is the way it has always been. In the heart of the group or at the edges you jostle for your turn. So.

When I was a child I spoke like a child, she thinks. But now I am grown, I may shout at the devil.

The past is waiting to happen again. This time I will make changes and stare her down, this time not in corridors or wasteland but in the sprawl of the modern work place, with its nuances and tensions and traps.

She'll take her on. Her mind is already running with the ways she can undermine and smear. Emails shared with everyone but her, impossible deadlines, directing her to the wrong rooms and ambiguous instructions. She dreams of the humiliations and petty vengeances that office life can provide, the futile tasks and soul-destroying repetitions and the silences. But in her heart she knows she may always be beaten and it is too late to even up her lost years and holding back a bonus and not inviting her to lunch have no equivalence to spit on the face and the echoing of an empty sports hall.

Angie had taken a time to work it out, but suddenly it all came back to her. She sat in a busy city centre bar, with her third drink untouched, biting her nails, smiling to herself, an afternoon unfolding with nothing to do but stoke herself up. She texted her friend and started to plan her next move.

Six months later Angie has settled in. She is reliable, punctual and has learned quickly. She and Jennifer have worked well together, neither has made reference to the past. Jennifer's early fantasies of revenge have petered out. Angie stays late, she has shown initiative and has suggested improvements, she comes in to Jennifer's office to ask if there is anything she can do to help. She makes Jennifer laugh and has proved generous when they have gone to the pub, with the rest of the office on Fridays.

But Angie has phoned in sick. Jennifer didn't take the call, but it seems she may be off for a while; Jennifer expects to receive a further message, maybe a text.

Then today she receives a letter. A solicitor encloses several sheets of supporting evidence and she reads the story of how Angie has been bullied, isolated, victimised and humiliated by Jennifer for the last six months. The letter says that Angle is receiving professional help after what is referred to as a breakdown. The letter is heavy with threat.

Jennifer is breathing hard; a phone rings in an adjacent office with the urgent insistence of the bell for assembly.

# Liar, Liar! Pants On Fire! – Joanne Derrick

'Liar! Liar!' they chanted before pushing me in a clump of stingers and running off.

I wasn't a liar. It was a true story. I'd heard Mum telling most of the women in the street as well as half our relatives when they descended on our house in Winfield Road.

I limped home in agony. Could you die from nettle stings? Probably. They might get infected and turn into seeping sores like old Mr Beddows had on his legs.

Mum was at the stove boiling cabbage when I got in.

'Billy! Where have you been till this time? Not crawling over those bomb sites again, I hope?'

I was a liar, wasn't I?

'No, Mam, honest.'

Then she noticed the tears. 'Billy, love. What on earth's the matter? What are those red blotches all over your face?'

I began to howl then. I woke my baby sister and she joined in. Mrs Foster would be banging the wall soon, even though she should be used to the racket we made in our house by now.

'They pushed me in the stingers, Mam. After I told 'em about me dad jumping out of that bomber.'

Mam ran upstairs and came back down with a big wad of cotton wool in a blue packet. She dipped it in Pond's Cold Cream every night to clean her face or summat, but now she was dabbing it with some 'orrible smelling stuff and smearing it over all my stings. I didn't feel right standing in our kitchen with nowt on, but she promised me no one would see.

Later, when I sat on the outside lav before bedtime, I thought about me da. Jumping out of a burning plane was the sort of thing he would do. He was brave and fearless. That's what me mam and me dad's brother told me when Da joined the RAF in 1939. He was a gunner and he'd be the best shot ever. Ack ack ack… shooting at those Jerry planes and making 'em fall from the sky. He was a hero, my da.

I took a sheet of newspaper from the rusty nail on the wall. Des Wallace had scribbled 'Kilroy was 'ere' on the newly whitewashed wall last week and me mam had about throttled him. Us kids spent hours after school finding as many 'Kilroy was 'ere' slogans as we could. The longer the war went on, the more we found.

Mam said it was my job to wind Da's old clock every day. She showed me how to do it just right to make sure I didn't overwind it. It had been his uncle's. The one who died in the trenches. Granny said he had to treasure it all his days and that it wasn't ever to stop 'cos if it did, then Uncle Fred's soul wouldn't rest. It was a big job, but Mam said I was the little man of the house now and that I was up to the task. Made me feel important, I can tell you. The other kids in the street think I'm a big 'ead. Even more now 'cos of the story about Da jumping out of his plane.

Before going up to bed, I carefully wound the clock. Ma looked up and smiled. She was knitting another pullover for me and listening to dance tunes on the radio with a smile on her face.

'I like to imagine your da and me dancing at the church hall after the war is over,' she said. 'Pity he wasn't injured just a little bit after that jump, then he'd have had to come home.'

As I lay in bed reading my Dandy comic, I thought about Da jumping out of that plane and how scared he must have been. They'd been on a raid over Germany. The Lancaster was hit by enemy fire and was in flames. There wasn't time to put on a parachute, so instead of burning to death, Da decided to jump. The plane was 18,000 feet up. He landed uninjured and conscious. He fell at a rate of 120mph and his fall was broken by the springy branches of pine trees and deep snow. Always been lucky, my Da.

'Liar! Liar! Pants on Fire!'

I could understand why the other kids didn't believe me, but I read the letter from Da's superior officer. Ma said she's going to frame it.

When I got up the next morning, Uncle Fred's old clock had stopped. The cold chill of the parlour snatched my breath and I shivered. What had I done wrong?

'Ma! Ma! The clock's stopped!'

But she wasn't in the house. She was at the gate. A lad was giving her a telegram. It was like watching Mrs Foster next door all over again. The shaking hands. The sob. Fainting. The telegram boy going bright red.

'Ma?'

I didn't have to read the telegram to know my da was dead. Killed in action.

Then I understood.

It was my fault.

I was so busy thinking about my da, the hero, that I'd overwound the stupid old clock. Uncle Fred 'Up In Heaven' had got mad and decided to punish us all, otherwise why else had my da been killed?

And I'd lied to Mum about playing on the bomb sites.

Liar! Liar! Pants On Fire!

I put my hands over my ears in an attempt to shut out the sound of the other kids' taunts and my ma's wailing sobs.

# Meteors – Jade Chen

We were friends for a long time until one day romantic feelings flowered unexpectedly between us. We didn't see it coming but when it did, it was one of the most natural processes I've ever experienced. Like the sun rising every day without fanfare, without fireworks, without fail. Those feelings crept up softly and burrowed their way through the innermost caves within me. I was amazed at how easily I surrendered myself to the flow of things without a single ounce of resistance that usually comes from the twin engines of rationality and fear. I was like a leaf in a river, flowing down where the currents lead me to on a fixed path I know not of. And for the first time in my life this surrender was effortless and painless on my part. I was content, strangely calm and light-hearted. All I felt was an overwhelming peace in my heart that I've never ever experienced before. The world felt ablaze with brand new possibilities and adventures. I was convinced these were signs that our relationship was something truly special.

We were walking together quietly back home after dinner and grocery shopping. We went crazy at the grocery store again, as usual, grabbing and shoving whatever tickled our fancy into our groaning baskets. And so now our arms paid the price of bearing the weight of four packets of mushrooms, two cartons of milk, two cartons of apple juice, two bags of chips, three aubergines, a packet of four chicken thighs, two thick slices of pork chops, a wedge of parmesan cheese, a tub of chocolate chip and mint ice cream and a block of butter (his); along with a tub of white miso, a slab of salmon, a bottle of *Kikkoman* soy sauce, sake, mirin and maple syrup, two organic dark chocolate bars, a packet of dried cranberries, unbleached white flour, four pears, two peaches, five lemons and a box of chocolate cookies (mine). We'd have an incredible feast in the coming days. But for now, we walked with laboured breaths.

I sighed miserably and muttered about the load under my breath, not intending him to hear too much of it for he was already carrying more than his share. He suddenly turned towards me and casually asked, 'Can I help you carry some of that?'

Turning towards him, I couldn't help but give a little gasp. It was dark and drizzling slightly. His face was half shrouded in shadow, half illuminated by the warm orangey light from the lamppost along the street. Looking at him up-close like this, the crease of his eyelids, the way his shoulders sloped downwards, his earnest eyes locked straight onto mine, all that came to my mind in that split second was: this is the face I want to be staring at forever.

He was still peering at me and waiting for a response. 'Uh, it's okay, baby. You're already carrying so much more', I stammered. I was blushing slightly but that was hardly visible to him under the dim lights. He nodded and suddenly smiled gleefully, 'Oh, I can't wait to have the ice cream when we get home. Mmm, mmmmm!' I laughed at his eager look of anticipation and we continued our slow walk home.


It was a warm and breezy Saturday afternoon. We were both reading languidly on the couch, him lying down with his head on my lap. Our glasses of iced green tea were sweating in the afternoon heat onto our table top.

'Sometimes I'll think of you and suddenly get the incredible urge to cry. You find it ridiculous don't you? Well, so do I! But it's not because I feel sad or my heart is broken. On the contrary, I get totally overwhelmed with gratitude, and the full magnitude of it all just hits me all at once. It's like stepping under the showerhead and getting utterly drenched. Like stepping out from the cool shade into the scorching sun. In that second I'm overwhelmed by all these physical sensations, one thought keeps appearing in my mind like words on the empty pages of a book: *I'm so lucky. I'm so lucky. Thank you, thank you. I'm so lucky. Thank you.* And I have to close my eyes to stop the tears from falling.

How many people search to the ends of this earth for their love? How many people are, right now, privately despairing that they'll never find them or be found? And yet here I am crying with gratitude, because I have you.'

I paused to catch my breath. I could feel his gaze on me, so I looked at him. He was utterly still although his expression was one of utmost tenderness. His eyes were soft and shiny with moisture. I had started telling him the most important lesson I've learnt, and I couldn't stop now.

'It's a wonderful, incredibly astounding, magical thing. The beauty of the universe explodes in my face, penetrates my entire being through the portal that is my heart and I'm connected to this universe, this essence, this life force that ties us, this earth, the galaxy and this grand, vast cosmos together. How this earth came into being was a miracle. The life that came into being on this earth is the second happy miracle. The more I think about it, the more I'm convinced and in awe of this: we're all made of stardust. And because of that, we're infinite. When we die, we become stardust again. The sheer potential and power of love was the life force that birthed this earth and humans into existence. This capacity to love, this innately human tendency and condition was what created us out of nothing. It's our very right to exist. All these feelings, all these thoughts came to me—all because you love me, and I love you. I thank you for this gift of sacred insight. I hold you, and your gift of love to me, sacred. And I'll guard it with my life for it *is* my life.'

I looked deeply into his eyes. Those familiar and mysterious depths that stare right back into me.

'Thank you for your love that has made me realise the essence of our existence. We love each other into existence, into being, into becoming, into our end. And even the end has no end. We'll exist in the infinite vastness of the stars and space until the next miracle, the next lifetime, the next adventure on this planet, or maybe another.'

He smiled and I could see the tears in his eyes. Tenderly, he brushed the tears that slipped down my cheeks in continuous streams, as tears ran down his. He held my hand tightly and we both cried, for our hearts were full and we couldn't love each other more than we did at this very moment.


Stars and planets, ephemeral life, space ad inifinitum.

We may be passing meteors in the grand passage of time, but look how brilliantly we shone together.

# No Cause For Concern – Alison Wassell

In the car, outside the client's house, Roz checks her phone. She has six missed calls, all of them from her mother's neighbour. Glancing at her watch she reluctantly makes a call. Mother has been 'up to her tricks' again, and the neighbour has had to take her in, for her own safety. It's the third time in a fortnight. The neighbour pauses here, and Roz moves her phone away from her ear as she senses her disapproval. Mother has removed all the light bulbs from their sockets. The neighbour discovered her, in her nightie and slippers, planting them in the garden.

'It can't go on,' says the neighbour. Roz promises to be there within the hour.

She has had no time to read the case notes. She picks up the ominously heavy file from the passenger seat and scans the first couple of pages. Her heart lurches as she spots a familiar name: Kevin Foster. She came across him years ago, before he went inside. She looks at her watch again. She doesn't have time for this.

She has a ladder in her tights. Attempting to ignore it, she strides purposefully towards the house. The door opens before she has had time to press the bell. Roz offers her identification tag.

'Pauline's off sick,' she says, by way of introduction. Silently, she curses her absent colleague.

Shelley, the client, appears dressed for an interview. Her white blouse is only slightly too tight, her skirt only a fraction too short. She totters on her heels as she leads the way into the living room. Roz hangs back, rummaging in her handbag. She takes a second to scrutinise the coats that are piled on a chair in the hallway. They appear to belong to a woman and two children. Roz ticks a mental box.

The older child complains as Shelley makes him turn off the blaring television. The younger one sucks her thumb as she clutches a naked Barbie doll. Shelley settles herself between them on the sofa and neatly crosses her legs. Roz perches on the edge of an armchair. She smiles at the boy.

'You must be Jack,' she says.

'Jake,' he corrects her. She feels herself shrinking under his contemptuous gaze.

'Silly me,' she says, slapping her wrist and giggling like a schoolgirl. This does nothing to improve matters. After a noticeable silence, Shelley smiles forgivingly. She asks Jake if he has any homework to do, nodding meaningfully at him as she speaks. Roz wonders how many times they have rehearsed this routine.

Jake sighs, slides reluctantly off the sofa and fetches a battered book bag, from which he produces two crumpled worksheets. Shelley examines them, her lips moving slightly as she reads. She returns the sheets to him, telling him to go and do them in his bedroom. As he leaves she turns to Roz.

'I don't know where he gets his brains from,' she says. Roz feels her phone vibrating in her pocket. Shuffling uneasily, she turns her attention to the little girl, who is now chewing Barbie's naked foot whilst twisting an already tangled lock of hair around her fingers. The words 'dishevelled appearance' form in Roz's mind. She pushes them away. Some children are incapable of staying tidy for more than five minutes. She needs this to be over quickly.

'I used to take all the clothes off my dollies too,' she tells the child, who stares blankly at her as she continues to twist and chew. Shelley nudges her, perhaps just a little too hard.

'The lady's talking to you, Kira. Where are your manners?' Kira scowls and turns away from her mother. She curls herself into a ball, burying her face in the arm of the sofa.

'Kids,' says Shelley, shaking her head in mock exasperation. Roz's phone vibrates again. She is clammy with anxiety, and can smell her own perspiration, despite the deodorant. She needs to move things on.

They should have a little chat, she tells Shelley. She suggests that Kira goes to play in her room. Shelley snorts.

Jake and Kira have to share a room, now that the council has rehoused them in this matchbox. She doesn't want Jake disturbed while he's doing his homework.

Leaving Kira and Barbie on the sofa they go through to the tiny kitchen. There is a strong smell of bleach. As Shelley fills the kettle they hear the television being turned back on. There is barely room for the two of them. Roz breathes in and presses her back into the edge of the worktop as Shelley squeezes past her to get to the fridge. As she takes out the milk Roz seizes the opportunity to look inside. It contains mainly ready meals. Not ideal, reflects Roz; but who is she to condemn someone for not cooking from scratch? Lately, she has been ordering takeaways, on the nights that she remembers to eat. The most important thing is that there are no beer cans. Kevin Foster, as she remembers, was always a big drinker.

Shelley produces two mugs of instant coffee. The steam from the mug clouds Roz's glasses. She sets it down and rummages in her pocket for a tissue to clean them. Her phone crashes onto the floor, beginning to vibrate again as it does so. It crawls along the slightly grubby vinyl.

'Don't you need to take that?' asks Shelley. Roz knows that humiliation will have turned her pink. She hurriedly stoops to retrieve the phone, and bangs her head on the worktop as she stands. Everything is fine, she insists. Whoever it is can wait. She switches off the phone and takes a long drink of too-hot coffee as she attempts to regain her composure.

Shelley is looking bored. She taps her perfectly manicured nails on the draining board as she waits. Roz swallows her panic and begins.

'So, how are things?' she says, lamely. Shelley shrugs, and doesn't bother to answer. She turns to pour what remains of her coffee down the sink, then crosses her arms across her chest. Roz takes a deep breath.

'I'm assuming you know Kevin's been released,' she says, as she studies Shelley's face. If she's a liar, she's a good one.

'What's that to me?' she asks, sounding as though she couldn't care less. This is good, thinks Roz. She forges on.

'It's just that there's been a report of him being seen around this area,' she says. Shelley is angry now. Roz recognizes the signs; the heavy breathing, the clenched fists, the pink spots that have appeared on her cheeks.

'It's that interfering old cow next door, isn't it?' snarls Shelley. She's right, but Roz says nothing. She waits, sipping the remains of her cooling coffee.

Shelley licks her lips several times before she speaks again. Her eyes flick around the room nervously, as though she fears someone else might be listening. She leans towards Roz, and her voice is little more than a whisper.

'It was just the one time, yeah? He came knocking on the door and I sent him packing. There's no way I'd let him near my kids. Christ, what do you take me for?'

Roz thinks she detects actual tears in Shelley's eyes. She places a comforting hand on her arm.

'Just let us know, if he tries to get in touch again,' she says. Shelley nods, her chin wobbling slightly.

Roz asks if she can 'pop to the loo', before she leaves. She cringes at her words as they leave her mouth.

'Top of the stairs, first on the right,' says Shelley.

Leaning on the locked door, Roz switches her phone back on. It rings.

'Rosalind, you need to come quickly. Your mother is very distressed. And she seems to have lost control of her bladder. She has had a little accident.'

In the background, Roz hears her mother crying. She ends the call without replying. She notes that there are only three toothbrushes in the jar on the windowsill.

On the landing she leans against the bannister and does some breathing exercises. The door of the children's bedroom is ajar. Jake lies on his bed, the worksheets tossed on the floor. Some kind of electronic device bleeps in his hands. Roz reassures herself with the phrase 'normal ten year old'.

At the door Roz smiles at Shelley, and reminds her that she knows where they are, if she needs any help. The gesture Shelley makes with her head may, or may not, be a nod of appreciation.

As the door closes behind her, Roz searches in her bag for her car keys. A shrill, unfamiliar voice floats through the open window.

'Mum, can Uncle Kevin come back, now the posh lady's gone?'

Roz's hands close around the elusive keys. Afterwards, when the shit has well and truly hit the fan, she will deny that the last thirty seconds ever happened. She has found no cause for concern.

# Pseudonym –
# Richard Anthony Dunford

That letter arrives in the post.

That letter you've received a thousand times before.

That letter you half want to just chuck straight in the bin.

That letter with those oh so familiar words… Only this time, those words are missing. They've been replaced with new words.

These new words are alien.

You have to read it three times over.

You have to slap cold water in your face to check you're not dreaming.

You've applied to funding schemes to turn your passion projects into reality so many times the rejection just bounces off you like a sponge.

'We thank you for taking the time to submit your proposal but unfortunately on this occasion we won't be recommending you for arts funding.'

You've read it so many times.

They always encourage you to submit further work in the future. I guess this covers all their bases. Your next submission could end up a masterpiece that defines a generation.

Tactical sympathetic disappointment is the order of the day.

'It's not right for us' or 'this isn't quite the direction we're going in at the moment' is not the damnation that you haven't an ounce of talent in your pathetic soul.

It's not the harsh dose of reality that will be ringing in your ears as you take a walk up to the roof of the tallest building you can find and step off the ledge.

Where are those familiar words?!

Where's the template rejection letter and the hollow best wishes for all your future endeavours.

Don't give up. We don't want the guilt of your spiral into a lifetime condemned to dead-end minimum-wage jobs on our conscience.

But when that letter arrives with new words you've never seen before. Words like acceptance.

Congratulations. Approved. Granted.

A sentence that begins with 'we're delighted to inform you…'

Well, you'll tell the interviewer in the retrospective documentary on your ascent to superstardom that you took it in your stride…but you know otherwise.

You know you did a silly dance.

You know you ran around the house screaming like a schoolgirl hyped up on fizzy drinks.

It's the greatest moment of your life.

All those art classes.

All those late nights.

All the double shifts stacking shelves in budget supermarkets to buy brushes, canvases and an easel that didn't collapse every two hours.

All the times you struggled to get the paint clean from underneath your fingernails and watched a rainbow of colours rinse down the plughole.

Suddenly it's all worth it.

And then in the blink of an eye the rug gets pulled out from under you.

There and then is when you remember.

You remember what you did.

You remember the form.

That bloody equal opportunities monitoring form.

You'd spent hours crafting applications before. Poured your heart and soul onto that page only to feel it sink once you reached the end and had to fill out the mandatory equal opportunities form.

They always say this form has no bearing on your application.

So why are you asking then?!

You were a heterosexual white male.

The epitome of the majority.

As soon as you ticked those boxes you might as well have erased every word that had come before.

Just once you think what the heck.

Just once you bend the rules.

You have this theory they have to give finance to certain criteria to appease the government and look fair, so just this once…you go wild.

Problem is, the one time you weren't completely honest with your application and told a couple of little white lies is the one time you get asked in for an interview.

Get asked to attend the contract signing in person.

Get asked to take publicity photos as you sign on the dotted line.

Get asked to make a personal appearance in front of the board of directors before the funding for your new art exhibition gets transferred into your bank account.

A bank account you now have to set up in a pseudonym as you couldn't use your real name for the application as that name had applied multiple times already.

Trouble is they're not expecting a heterosexual white male to walk through those doors.

The people who can change your life forever and finally give you the funding to take your work to the next level…they're expecting a transgender bisexual from an ethnic minority with a disability to enter that room.

You know it's wrong but you don't want to wave goodbye to that money.

You know it's wrong but you grow a beard and dress up like a drag queen.

You know it's wrong but you paint your own skin and practice an accent.

You know it's wrong but you buy a wheelchair off eBay and inject your legs with a sedative just in case you lose concentration at the interview.

You know it's wrong but this is the opportunity you've been waiting for your whole lifetime.

And when you get in front of that board of directors the last person in the world you wanted to see is sitting centre stage.

The one you dated through university.

The one you sat up late with night after night talking about how together you'd take the art world by storm.

The one who knows you better than anyone on the planet.

The one you insisted was the most beautiful girl you'd ever seen so she'd give you a blow job even though she'd told you the thought of performing oral sex made her stomach churn.

The one you gave the boot after the chick who you really thought was the most beautiful girl in the world gave you her number when you flirted outside a local takeaway.

That one. She's staring right into your lying, deceitful eyes as you try and convince the board you're disabled, from an ethnic minority and in the middle of a sex change.

You know she knows who you are.

You know she knows you're a big fat liar.

You know any moment she'll expose you.

Any moment you're gonna officially be the worst human being alive and hated by each and every minority you've exploited for your own selfish gain.

For a moment you think to yourself if only you'd stuck with her maybe she'd have got you the funding you longed for.

Maybe you could offer to lick her out in return for some decent paints and a workspace to develop new ideas.

You wait for that moment…but it never comes.

For some reason she keeps silent.

For some reason she lets you pull off the pretence.

For some reason she lets you sign on that dotted line.

And finally you've won. Finally you have the money you've always needed to dedicate your life to your art.

Before you know it your face is in magazines.

Before you know it your work's revered by collectors around the world.

Before you know it those original paintings you would've sold for a week's rent are being fought over at auction and going for seven figures.

Before you know it you're a household name…only it's not your name.

It's your pseudonym.

Paranoid you'll get discovered you get your skin permanently bleached and book in for the sex change operation.

Paranoid you'll get caught out you pay a homeless drunk to cripple your legs with a baseball bat.

Paranoid your whole world will come crumbling down you hire a hit man to take out the one person who knows the truth.

As the years go by you forget your real name altogether.

You embrace the pseudonym.

You become the pseudonym.

You become a living, breathing piece of art.

And you paint.

It's the life you've always wanted.

So it didn't go quite how you originally imagined.

So you had to tell a few white lies to get where you needed to be.

You said you'd do anything to live your dreams…and you meant it.

# Starry, Starry Night –
# Meganne Hearne

Blood everywhere. Ray's mind whirled—he had better clear it up quickly, Margaret hated mess in the kitchen. He laughed: a choked, humourless sound. Backing into the living-room, the blood untouched, Ray shuddered. He collapsed when his legs touched the sofa, his hands balled, his body rocking gently. He could still see the kitchen scene, distorted and grotesque, through the Flemish glass door.

Ray heard the keening, unaware that it issued from him; neither did he feel any pain as his fingernails gouged his palms. He had to do something, oh God, but what? His fists pounded his knees in long-contained anger and frustration. This time he acknowledged his voice as it rose to an anguished roar, not ceasing until it ran hoarse.

Spent, Ray sagged on the sofa, his mind beginning to function once more. Reluctantly he rose and crossed the mile of carpet to the kitchen. Margaret's body still lay on the floor, her knees up and arms curled inward like a child. If it wasn't for the blood, Ray could almost believe that he hadn't really ended forty-three years of marriage with one knife-thrust.

The frying pan sizzled, filling the small room with the smell of burnt onions. With a great effort, he dragged his eyes away from Margaret to the smoking pan. For a flicker of a second, a thought burned itself into Ray's brain: a cleansing fire would be so easy. No, he thought, the police could never be fooled by such a childish attempt. Even if the evidence itself didn't scream 'murderer', Ray doubted he could lie convincingly.

Inching forward, Ray shuffled until his feet were as close as he could get to Margaret without actually touching her. Bracing himself against the counter, he extinguished the gas and realised he had been holding his breath.

If Margaret were here now, he could imagine just what she would say: 'You're a weak, worthless fool, Raymond Leith—you can't even keep a clean kitchen.' Ray caught himself and choked back a sob. He staggered to the doorframe and clung on, his knuckles white, until his strength returned.

Ray felt bile rise in his throat, tried desperately to contain it, clasped his hands across his mouth, raced across the living room, up the stairs and into the bathroom. He disgorged until he felt he must be purging his very soul.

Finally reduced to dry heaves, Ray dropped the toilet seat out of habit and flushed. Leaning heavily on the basin, he stared at his reflection in the mirrored cabinet. With a fury he did not know he possessed, Ray slammed his fist into the cabinet and a web of cracks spidered across the mirrored door. Marching from bathroom to bedroom, Ray swept ornaments and pictures to the floor.

Taking a deep breath—Margaret really wouldn't like this—Ray dug his fingers under the linen of the pristine double bed and heaved at it with such force that the mattress lifted and fell back askew, the pillows flopping onto the floor. His hands relaxed their white-knuckle grip on the sheets, he sank to the floor and cried.

They had never been blessed with children; whilst Ray had never held this against Margaret, he had sensed in her a sullen resentment. He had tried so hard to please, had taken her wild fury, sour criticisms and physical torments with a meekness that had epitomised their relationship. He had no idea that forty-three years had filed his frustrations to such a sharp point.


Thinking back on the events of the evening, Ray could find no explicit decision to stab Margaret. Even as he had raised the knife, it had been in a pleading thrust rather than an attack, an intention to push her away before her hand could issue another stinging slap. It had taken surprisingly little force to travel through her flesh, under her ribs, into her lung.

He knew it had gone into her lung because blood had immediately bubbled from her mouth, spattering as she issued drowning gasps. Letting go, he had watched in disbelief as she sank to her knees. Ray had been instantly paralysed, unable to move until Margaret had fallen where she now lay and the blood had ceased to pool from her mouth.

Now, slumped against the bed, Ray knew it was over. No more would he have to endure her rattling torments, her verbal and physical assaults. He could leave a can of beans on the kitchen counter all night and it wouldn't matter. It was over.

In desperation, Ray had sought help from his doctor six months previously. He had advised Ray that a marriage often seemed different after retirement and prescribed antidepressants and sleeping tablets. Pulling his pyjamas from the nightstand, Ray found the bottles where he had left them, hidden underneath. Slipping them into his trouser pocket, Ray walked downstairs.

Trancelike, he entered the kitchen, moving carefully around Margaret, to fill the kettle. While he waited for it to boil, he set out a cup and saucer and added a teabag. He flicked the kitchen radio on to kill the silence. 'Starry, Starry Night': their song. Ray switched it off with a grunt.

He finished making his tea and, almost as an afterthought, took a can of beans from the cupboard and stood it neatly beside the kettle. Returning to the living-room, Ray sat in his usual chair and withdrew the tablet bottles from his pocket. He snapped the cap off, tipped out two tablets and swallowed them with a sip of tea. He tipped out two more, then another two. Calmly, he swallowed them also, and began to hum the song he had been so keen to silence.

When Ray had neither tablets nor tea left, he remained in his seat, unconcerned, silently mouthing the words:

*'Starry, starry night.*
*Paint your palette blue and grey,*
*Look out on a summer's day,*
*With eyes that know the darkness in my soul.'*

# Stopping In – Diane Simmons

The dribble of saliva trickling down his chin wakes Ted a few seconds before he hears his name being called. He opens his eyes and wipes his mouth before scanning the room for clues to his whereabouts. After taking in the rows of chairs, the drinks machine, the porter pushing a patient on a trolley, he nods at his son. 'Have you finished, lad? Did the doctor get a good look at your knee?' he asks.

'Yes, no problems.' Ian gets up. 'You look done in, Dad. Did you get as far as the precinct?'

Ted pulls himself up, dusts biscuit crumbs off his trousers. 'I didn't bother—plenty going on here without going to the shops.'

'You just sat here?' Ian looks at his watch. 'But I've been gone two hours.'

'I had a cup of tea and a biscuit.'

'I thought the point of you coming with me to Preston was for you to have a look round.'

'I wasn't fussed. It was you that mentioned the shops. I was just glad of the outing—better than stopping in.'


The doorbell wakes Kathy. She's no idea how long it's been ringing—the noise from it having been incorporated into her complicated dream—and she almost stumbles into the hall. She stands for a moment, assesses her appearance in the mirror, brushes cake crumbs off her jumper before she opens the door. She smiles when she sees it is her daughter.

'Sorry,' Kathy says. 'I must have fallen asleep.'

'I can see that, Mother—you look a right state.'

Kathy runs her fingers through her unruly hair and pushes it behind her ears. She tries, as usual, not to mind her daughter's abruptness. 'Well you look nice anyway,' she says with a smile. 'Your hair all tied up in a plait—come through.'

'I can't stop, work's really full on, but I thought you might like to try this new artichoke quiche I've started doing,' she says, walking through into the living room. Rachel looks around. 'You've not been watching daytime television, Mother? And why were you asleep? Have you not been sleeping at night? I—'

'I just dozed off. And I enjoy a bit of television. It's not a crime.'

Ted takes the tin foil container out of the fridge and lifts off the cardboard lid. He's hungry after his outing to the hospital, but the casserole Ian's made him looks unappetising—grey pieces of turkey floating in a thin tomato sauce. When he spots a couple of stray tomato stalks he wrinkles his nose, wraps the container in a plastic bag and shoves it to the bottom of the bin. Finding nothing to tempt him in the fridge, Ted rummages through the freezer hoping to find a steak pie or macaroni cheese—something rich. Ian's been brilliant at making him home-cooked food since Irene died last year, but the low-fat meals Ian likes aren't to Ted's taste really. Sighing, he shuts the freezer door and reaches for the frying pan.

Kathy eats all the artichoke quiche in one go. She'd intended to cut it in half, perhaps have it with a bit of salad, but when she looks in the fridge she sees that the lettuce has gone gooey in its bag and the cucumber has turned to mush. She doesn't even heat the quiche up or set the table, just sits down on the sofa in front of *The One Show* and devours it.

When she's finished eating she plonks the plate on the coffee table and sighs. It feels good to eat something homemade. She's a good cook, Rachel, no doubt about it. She gets that from her, of course, but since her husband died two years ago, Kathy can't be bothered to do much cooking. As part of her grieving spending spree she'd bought a new oven not long after John died, but she's rarely switched it on.

Ted's up early the next day. Saturday's the day Ian and he go to the pub for lunch and he likes to have time to take a long bath and spruce up his clothes. He's struggling to iron a crease in his best trousers when the doorbell rings. Annoyed at being interrupted, his mood changes when he sees Ian through the glass panel of the front door. 'Come in, lad, come in,' he says. 'You're early!' Ian follows his dad through to the lounge and perches on the arm of a chair.

'Sorry, Dad, I'm afraid I'm not going to be able to make lunch.'

'Eh?'

'I've managed to get myself a date, with the woman I met last month, you know, the one I liked. She's always so busy and…well, I didn't want to miss the opportunity.'

'The woman with the hair?'

Ian laughs. 'Yes, the woman with the hair.'

Ted flops down onto the settee. 'Oh well, I can't compete with a date.'

'You could go to the pub anyway.'

'On my own? Don't be daft!'

'There's sure to be people you know.'

'I'll just stop in.'

Ian gets up and pats Ted on the shoulder. 'I'd best go. I don't want to be late.'

'No, well, you mustn't keep a lady waiting.'

'It would be good for you to get out and meet new people too, Dad.'

'So you keep saying.'

Ian shrugs. 'Have a look at those leaflets will you—I left them on the hall bookcase last time I came.'

Kathy's read the bistro menu twice and almost finished her glass of wine by the time Rachel walks through the door. She's been embarrassed sitting in the busy bistro alone, but as soon as Rachel arrives Kathy forgives her. Rachel looks so pretty in her casual linen clothes, her auburn hair loose for once. Rachel leans over and kisses Kathy on the cheek. 'I'm so sorry, the phone wouldn't stop ringing.'

'You're here now. And looking lovely.'

Rachel takes off her jacket. 'I don't feel it.'

'Were they work calls?'

'Yes, four potential new clients this morning!'

'Oh, that's good, love.'

'Well it would be, but—'

Kathy picks up the menu. 'Shall we have the lasagne?' she asks.

While they wait for their food, they chat, or at least Rachel does. Kathy feels dull; unable to think of anything that will interest her daughter. When their lasagne arrives, Kathy takes a few mouthfuls and pulls a face. 'This is disappointing today—it's not nearly as good as yours.'

Rachel laughs. 'It's your recipe I use!'

'True. Still, it's nice to be out!'

Rachel puts down her knife and fork and looks directly at Kathy. 'Oh, Mum, I can't stand the thought of you in that flat all day. Have you thought anymore about what I suggested? You don't want to end up like Grandma, sitting on her bum for hours on end.'

'She did a lot of knitting!'

Rachel laughs and takes a large gulp of merlot. 'I can't believe you're defending Grandma.'

'It's not so cut and dried when you get older.'

'You're sixty-one, Mum, not ninety-one. Even if what I suggested doesn't appeal, you still need to do something to get out of the house—sewing classes or French, anything…'

Ted's relieved when he answers his front door. The woman is older than he'd imagined but she's got a pleasant face and kind eyes. She smiles at him. 'Mr Robinson?' she asks.

'Call me Ted. You must be Kathy.'

He leads her through to the kitchen. It looks nice since he gave it a good clean. The whole house looks better for his efforts and he wishes he'd done it sooner, feels ashamed of his neglect. 'Have you done much of this?' he asks.

Kathy places her bag on the table and looks round the room. 'Not a great deal,' she says. 'Well, to be honest this is my first time.'

Ted rubs his hands together and grins. 'We're in this together then. It's my son that gave me the idea. He's been on at me for ages.'

'My daughter's the same. She's been asking me to help out with her business for a while now, but well…' She shrugs. 'I lacked the confidence somehow.'

'It's your daughter's business?'

Kathy nods. 'I'm so proud of her. She only started up a year ago, but she's inundated with customers. It must be all those television programmes!'

'There are a lot of them! Shall I put the kettle on..?'

'Perhaps later. Do you want to wash your hands and then we can get on. I'll just unpack everything,' she says, emptying the contents of her bag on to the table. When she's finished, Ted picks up one of the plastic bags up and smiles.

'Is that steak?' he asks.

'Stewing steak,' she says, handing him an apron. 'I thought we'd start with a steak and ale casserole— something easy for your first lesson.'

# The Art Expert's Child –
# Jenifer Granger

By a quiet creek of a river in China is a villa within a walled compound where the women of the family spin threads from golden cocoons. The tidal water with celadon-coloured light comes so close to the villa it reaches a string of reeds and a few pebbles lying on the shore. Farther away, banks of sand and reeds emerge through a haze that screens the open river up to a distant foam-rimmed edge.

The compound is loosely and clumsily divided into raised courtyards linked by three or four stone steps. Trees on each courtyard, with leaves a variety of shapes: rounded palm, elongated pine, splay-fingered banana, grow no shadows, yet their roots, a fine mesh, grip the soil at the foot of the walls or pull away from a height. A side-arch in a stone wall gives a glimpse like cloisonné of fretted rooms and open spaces leading onto each other in and out of sight.

The scene is painted on two sheets of bamboo paper.

On one sheet, beneath a slatted shelter held up by stickpoles, the spinners tend a jar of golden cocoons. A single thread climbs high in the air over a slender beam before running down to a wooden wheel.

On the other, two friends with a looped skein chat a moment on a lower courtyard while in the pavilion a gust catches a curtain where a woman waits beside a reel for the winding onto bobbins to continue. A console is set with a teapot and bowl.

Heads of visitors bob over the compound wall and inside a small boy about four years old, watched over by a woman, stands on a bench holding up his arms.

It is a day like other days. There are down-to-earth mosses and weeds in angles, large prickly spines on tree trunks, a spray of dirty droplets spilt on the soil, and dust and rain have streaked the walls, yet the long skirts of the spinners brush the ground where they glide, on unseen feet.

*Rue des Antiquaires, Angers.* I park my car under the chestnut trees where an ancient wall rises a blind fifty feet and, placing a ticket from the meter at my windscreen, I cross for a quick visit to the shops. Over the years, a foreigner and art amateur in this town in the Loire valley, I have come to know the antique dealers. They are casual, canny professionals, instructive but not talkative. Their outlook, not wary of strangers, is indifferent to the passage of time. Their collections of odd objects from different countries have washed up, their histories lost also.

The afternoon light breaks into the den. In the dead silence there seems to be no one. At the back, behind a massive desk piled ceiling high with books and objets d'art: bronzes, bells, bowls, Buddhas, bibelots, and barely visible in the clouds of *Gitanes* smoke, a nod of the head no words indicates Monsieur Perano, *Expert d'Art*, seated low, has acknowledged my presence. Art collectors take the train from as far as Paris to seek his opinion on oriental subjects: his taste in a fanholder to bid for at Drouot's, his advice about a collection of Chinese *lianhuanhua*, 'By The Waterside' booklets. He does not deal in fakes. Artworks are his life's passion.

'Call the firemen,' I say before I proceed to navigate around the high silhouetted central island blocking most of the interior. The route off to the right is a cul de sac completely choked up with jumbled furniture, frames, cardboard boxes and a cupboard.

Around the central island are 19th century Barbizon oils and African sculptures suggesting rituals exorcising fears, projecting desire for power, one a mask of blood-clotted feathers and bone, but chiefly oriental works detailed and luminous, cabinets of shadow, pointed ivory or metal objects in a flat glass case. On the walls, an occasional daguerreotype of a pin-up embracing a raised leg or in leaning-back posture and an old portrait of Jane Birkin show the proprietor has a taste for the lovelies.

An arresting oil catches my eye. I hesitate. It has no light, no hope in it.

A gun-metal grey bridge blocks the sky at the vertical above the unlit water eddying past its pillars, the current being slow and deep. The shore widens beyond and rounds an arm. In the distant sunset it could hold the lights of a city. In the arch's shadow, isolated in the middle of gangrenous green and vivid yellow water, is a small, black boat-shed reached by a pontoon. A place for a piss, a pit, a suicide.

'Can I look closer at this, please?' I ask, and Monsieur Perano giving his permanent smoker's cough, his eyelids lowered, comes out from behind his desk. Despite his bright tie, he looks paler than usual and his side-on smile is only an attempt at turning on charm.

Between thumb and index he holds up the painting to the light for me.

'It's a black hole, a hellhole,' I say.

'It is well-painted.'

'It's expensive for such a small thing.'

'I have to earn my living.' His voice is cracked pottery. 'I have a son to think of.'

'You have a son?'

'Yes, I have a son. Does that surprise you?'

Tucked away in his Ali-Baba's grotto, I had seen the art expert as a piece of art himself. Of course he must have an ordinary life outside, and if a child, then a wife and family. They had never been in the picture here before. I am on the point of leaving but give a second quick look around taking in the objects I have already seen, when I suddenly come across what I have been looking for.

On a low table in the dim light is a diptych painted on two sheets of bamboo paper.

A small boy grows up in a family of women who spin threads from golden cocoons by a river in China whose tide comes so close to the villa it weaves on the shore a string of reeds and a few pebbles. Fretted rooms and open spaces lead onto each other in and out of sight. This time, I do not question the price.

'In this case, I am sure of its true value,' says Monsieur Perano. 'It is complete.' And he passes me the pair of pictures.

'I shall frame them with a single reed of wicker,' I say to him.

'You, you can come here,' he says. And he calls me 'Jane Birkin'.

Further down the street, at the bric-à-brac *Les Caprices du Temps*, Mme. Caron the proprietor, shaking her *Napoléon III* bangles, recounts in a hushed voice to an acquaintance,

'The other day, Monsieur Perano shouted at a client!'

'He has been known to push unwelcome visitors out of the door,' says her friend.

Monsieur Perano is heading for the chemist's as I drive away. In a surge of friendship for him, I cannot help waving cheerily.


Occupied with building an extension to my country house, I have not forgotten that small despairing oil. I am about to return to the *Rue des Antiquaires* to take another look at it—somehow afraid it might have gone—when I notice, passing in the car, that Monsieur Perano's shop is shut, the iron curtain down. I make haste to park, cross over and there see the FOR SALE sign.

Monsieur Lelièvre hanging in the neighbouring doorway of his *Anges et Démons Antiquités* shakes his head.

'Monsieur Perano? Gone away? Dead. He died suddenly two weeks ago.'

We stare at each other, both of us shocked and at a loss. 'He probably didn't ask for help when he needed it. He wouldn't have,' says the antique dealer.

'He must have smoked himself to death.'

'Tobacco, insomnia, drink…'

'He was still a young man.'

'Divorced. He left behind a four-year-old boy.' The antique dealer's voice breaks.

'He cared a lot about his son.'

'His wife had gone away. He was the child's sole carer.'

'Who is going to take care of his child?' I ask. 'That is the question.'

M'sieur Perano had sisters. He came from a family of women who would bring the child up among them. There was no problem there.

A new shop they say is due to open in the *Rue des Antiquaires*. It will sell modern chinoiseries, padded jackets, sprayed polychromes, blue-and-white tea sets, attracting interest. The antique dealers one after the other I foresee will sell out, divorce, or turn to different affairs. The soul of the provincial town's street, aged in the light and shade of its ancient stones, has gone.

The diptych hangs in my extension.

I see at the same time, for a moment, in the interlude— outside the veranda window—the olive tree by the terrace, the white chairs and table.

# The Expediter – James Starke

He had seen them more than once during the past several weeks on his afternoon and evening strolls in the neighbourhood that took him past their house. They were newcomers to the area, he surmised. They seemed self-contained, inseparable even; a girl of about seven and a boy of five or so. He couldn't recall ever seeing them play with other children. Though apparently just typical kids, they seemed to keep their distance behind closed doors and drawn curtains most of the time. Maybe they were occupied with their electronic toys, and rarely forsook their rooms for outdoor play in their yard or in the nearby park. When they did appear outside he noted how attractive the children were, with dark hair and blue eyes. Their clothes were of good quality and always clean and neat. They always responded politely, if not shyly, when he greeted them on his solitary walks.

Due to a childhood accident in the rough-and-tumble of the district where he spent his early years, the absence of one of his eyes lent an almost sinister air to his face. Some commented that his facial configuration combined with his taciturnity and inscrutableness made him appear to be a player of poker, or some other game of chance. Despite his appearance, the man's greetings encouraged the children and over time the boy and girl came to accept him as a fixture in their immediate environment.

'Hello, mister, do you live near here?' the little girl asked him. He hesitated in his responses, not wanting to seem too friendly, considering the stories of crimes and kidnappings that fill the screens and newspapers almost daily. But on this day he paused and chatted.

'Why yes, I live just up the street in the red brick building with the big tree in front.'

'What's your name, mister?' the little boy asked. At first taken aback, the man reverted to his own childhood and answered as he might have done as a ten year old: 'Puddin' Tame, ask me again, and I'll tell you the same.'

He recalled that in his youth he also had another fall-back response: 'John Brown, ask me again and I'll knock you down.' This one he spared the children.

'Oh, that's funny, mister.' The little girl giggled.

'Hey, Puddin Tame, that's not a name,' the boy said with a puzzled look as if he'd just figured it out.

'You're right,' the man said, with a tight grin that showed worn-down nicotine-browned teeth and forced a squint over the false eye.

'My name is Ben,' he responded, snatching at the first name that came to mind, farthest from his own. As he was about to ask them their names, a woman's voice called for them to 'get into the house right now, children'.

His next encounter with them was in the park, several blocks from their house. They were sitting alone on a bench at the side of the lake, watching the progress of the various ducks and geese, but also crows and pigeons, in the now cooler late-summer afternoon. The little boy rocked back and forth, moaning with what might pass for chocolate ice cream streaming down his face, as it mingled with his tears and the fluids coursing from his nostrils.

He knew he mustn't reveal that he'd discovered the boy's name when he asked, 'What's wrong there, sport, did you lose something?'

'My ice cweam,' he lisped between sobs.

'He was shooing a bird away and he swung his sugar cone too hard and the ice cream fell out and the large birds snatched it away,' his sister's staccato voice reported the news in a most officious way.

'Well maybe I can help,' the man said, reaching into his pocket as he walked toward the ice cream kiosk. 'What flavour do you like?' he asked.

'Chocolate, pwease,' the boy answered, as he brightened up, while running a sleeve across his face.

'And by the way, what is your name?' the man asked, realising it was time to personalise their relationship.

'Spencer,' the boy replied through the arm still passing over his mouth and nose, further mingling what had collected on his face. But now the tears had dried up and a smile appeared like the sun through a dark cloud. As the man ordered the chocolate cone for Spencer, he asked the little girl for her name.

'Claire,' she said. 'It's really Ann Claire, but I prefer just the Claire part.'

'Would you like another cone?' he asked.

'No thanks,' she said. 'Mine didn't fall. We're not supposed to talk to strangers, because we're hiding from someone. Our dad is anyway,' she volunteered.

As he handed Spencer his cone, the man noticed a rapid movement out of the corner of his eye. He cursed his lack of attention and steeled himself in preparation for what might come. But as the form approached, a woman's nervous, high-pitched voice called out for his new friends.

'Claire, Spencer, what are you doing? You must not accept things from strangers,' she said, reaching for the cone. But when her eyes fell upon the one-eyed man, a moment of recognition passed over her face and a noticeable weight fell from her upper body, as a hint of a smile started to form.

'Oh, hello, you're the man from up the block who talks to the kids on your walks.' She thrust her hand out in a handshake. That gesture seemed to override the fear he had heard in her voice. 'Sarah,' she said as she pressed the man's hand.

'Ben. Spencer had a problem with his cone, so I bought him a new one. I hope that's all right,' he said with a smile that worked to offset the sagging tissue around his false eye.

'Of course, thank you,' she said as she brushed off the bench and sat down.

'As you can imagine, we try to instruct our children to avoid contact with strangers. It's the world we live in, you know.'

The man had the impression that the children's mother could have talked at length about her child raising, or about anything, for that matter.

'Can I get you something?' he offered. 'A coffee, perhaps?'

'No, nothing, thanks. We'll have to be going soon. But thanks for the kind offer.'

He sat down on the bench and watched with amusement as Spencer negotiated the large cone while his face took on even more shades of brown. Claire got up to chase some Canadian geese and Spencer joined in, this time carefully holding his cone with both hands.

'I don't mean to pry,' said the man, 'but Claire mentioned that their father, your husband, was in hiding, as she called it.'

'Oh my heavens,' she cried. 'That girl is going to be the…And Chad will be furious.'

'I'm sorry. I'll leave if you want,' he said.

'No, no, it's not your fault. You see my husband is an expediter. Anyway, that's what he calls himself. He was involved in some accounting improprieties. At least that's how he describes them. The Justice Department has moved us around because Chad is preparing to testify…' She said as her voice dropped off.

'That's way over my head,' the man said with a half smile that showed his brown lower teeth.

'I'm a retired expediter of sorts myself, I suppose one could say. What you describe are the kinds of things one reads about in novels and the occasional movie.'

'I wish that were the case with me and the kids,' she smiled through perfect teeth with a sparkle in her light blue eyes. She seemed a lot more relaxed as she talked more about life before her husband's problems.

'Will you excuse me?' the man asked after a glance at his watch. 'I have to use the men's room. I'll be right back.'

The park was crowded that day and there was an unusually long wait for the men's facilities. He brought out his cell phone and selected a prearranged number. As he finished washing and drying his hands, he heard the screech of tires and car doors slamming, which overrode all the other sounds of the park. A high-pitched, anguished woman's scream and the cry of a child soon followed.

Pushing his way through the waiting men to the restroom's exit, he made out the red brake lights on a black car disappearing out of the park's driveway. His eyes raked the bench where a large sugar cone lay, its brown contents scattered and squashed.

At that moment his cell phone rang. The familiar voice whispered the three words he was expecting, 'We have them.' The man's lips curled up over his brown teeth to form a smile as he closed the phone. He shook his head in amusement as he watched large black crows fending off smaller birds as they swarmed to the prize of the spilled ice cream cone.

# The Faraday Cage – Graeme Hall

The rain was easing slightly but the thunderstorm was getting closer. She found herself counting the seconds between the flash and the sound. What was it they said? One second was equal to one mile? She counted five seconds.

Parked directly underneath the pylon they were protected from the electrical storms that were all around them, and if the winds were to bring down the pylon it wouldn't fall on them. That was his theory anyway. She was sceptical but then she hadn't really wanted to come in the first place.

'You want us to go camping on the moors?'

'Not camping, I've told you; I'll borrow a camper van. It'll be like old times.'

In the end she had given in and here they were in a camper van in a thunderstorm. She wished she'd paid more attention to her physics lessons at school. The rain was being blown against the windows and there was a leak around the door. When the wind gusted the van rocked on its wheels. They should have blocked them with stones but neither of them wanted to go out to do it now. It was only early evening but the dark storm clouds made it seem later.

'Can't we just go home?' she said.

'In this weather? We're safer here.'

Catch-22 she thought.

They both knew why they were there. It was a final attempt to salvage something. Anything. Three weeks ago, in bed, they had had the conversation that she had dreaded but knew was inevitable.

'Who is it? Do I know him?' he had asked.

'No,' she answered.


She should have left then. She knew that now but he had played on her sense of guilt and she felt obliged to go through the motions of giving it another go. He reminded her that it had been seven years, so she owed him that much. Perhaps she did. What followed was a desperate effort to recreate the past. But of course it didn't work. How could it when the thought of the unnamed was always between them? This trip, an echo of their first summer together, was the one last try.

Another lightning flash. Two seconds then the thunder.

She would leave him when they got back. She was determined on that now but until then there was still this storm to get through. Within the van though everything was surprisingly calm. No ranting and shouting, no recriminations, only sadness. Sadness was the one final thing that they shared.

'It hasn't worked has it?' he said.

'What hasn't?'

'This trip.'

'Did you really think it would?'

Before he could answer, a lightning flash and thunderclap came that were too close for her to count the gap.

'Are you sure we're safe?' She was beginning to wonder if he had an ulterior motive.

'Of course. Provided we stay in here. Trust me on this at least.'

A gust of wind hit the van so violently that she was thrown into him.

'At least the elements are on my side,' he said. 'Perhaps the gods are trying to tell you something.' She moved away embarrassed by the unintentional intimacy.

'If I didn't know better I might think you've summoned up this storm yourself.'

'Like Prospero? If only. Then I could trap you here like Caliban. Or is it Ariel? I can never remember.'

She gave him a glance trying to see if he was joking but she couldn't read his expression.

An intense light filled the van in an instant and currents of blue ran across the windows while the air split with a crack. One of the windows shattered throwing shards of glass over them and when the light had gone they were left in darkness.

'Christ!' she exclaimed. 'What the fuck was that?'

'Are you OK?'

'I think so.' She started to pick fragments of glass out of her hair trying not to cut herself in the process. 'How come we're unhurt?'

'I told you,' he said, 'we're safe in here. Just us two together. It's outside that is dangerous.'

He flicked a switch off and on to no effect. He found a couple of torches and set them up to provide some light, and then found a picnic table that he used to cover the broken window.

'It's almost romantic,' he said.

'No it isn't. Did you plan this?' For the first time she was angry.

'What? Plan the storm? Getting hit by lightning?'

'Sorry. I'm just freaked out.'

He went to put an arm around her shoulder but she shook him off.

'No,' she said.


The storm continued but she was relieved to realise that a space was opening up again between the lightning and the thunder, and slowly the storm was passing away.

'There's nothing we can do until morning,' he said, 'we might as well try and get some sleep.'

Still dressed she curled up on one of the bunks and covered herself as best she could; in spite of the picnic table, rain was still getting in through the broken window. She slept fitfully and in her dreams she was in a boat tossed around in a storm before being shipwrecked on an island shore. When she woke it was daylight. The storm had gone and she could see the damage that the strike had done to the van. Parts were charred and there was a faint smell of ozone and burnt rubber. A teapot lay shattered on the floor but she noted that the lid was somehow still intact.

He was trying unsuccessfully to start the engine.

'Will it start?'

He turned towards her. 'No. It's completely dead. It seems we're stuck here.'

'I'll walk.' She rummaged around to find her boots and put them on.

'It's miles to the next village.'

'I don't care. I'm going.'

'But don't you understand? It's safe here. We're safe here together.'

She looked at him and saw only incomprehension. She turned away, opened the door and stepped out from the van.

# The Jogger In The Park – Kevin Brooke

I remember the last time you ran past me. Your blonde ponytail was bobbing up and down, following the rhythm of your steps. We shared a mutual smile. Not a lingering smile but tangible and enough to provide me with an emotional contentment for a few precious moments. I wanted to say thank you. Instead I tried to capture the moment, keep it safe. It was a mistake and I know I should've asked before I took your photograph. You looked so angry, shocked and I realised straight away that I'd crossed the line.

You used to go past my bench at the same time each day. Sometimes you'd stop. I don't blame you. It's a beautiful spot, where the fir tree canopy provides shelter from the elements and so unlike the rest of the park, which is so exposed. In the summer, of course, there's the added bonus of the sweet smell of pine intermingled with the sunshine.

Occasionally, you added a few words.

'Lovely morning,' you'd say or something about the weather. Warm, friendly words that would mean little to others, but to me they meant everything. You always seemed busy and even when you spoke you wouldn't pause completely, instead continuing to jog up and down on the spot, your eyes gazing around and taking in the view as though for the first time. Then you'd nod and carry on along the gravelled path in the direction of the stream.

Sometimes I can hear the water lapping against the rocks if the wind blows in a certain direction and if I'm lucky I get to see a blue flash and a glimpse of red as a kingfisher races past. A blur of colours blue and red, red and blue—the same colours I saw when the world stopped spinning and when anything and everything ceased to exist.

It was after the day I mentioned earlier, when I invaded your privacy and took your photograph that you stopped running past me. I never for one second truly believed you ran past my bench because of me, but I know for definite it was because of me that you changed your route and started running on the other side of the park.

I missed you. At first I thought there was something wrong, maybe you were unwell or even worse and I couldn't bear not knowing. So I found your address and that's how I was there when you came out of your front door—there's no other reason. You were easy to find. Everybody is unless they go to incredible lengths to make themselves invisible. It was good to see you. You didn't seem in the mood for company, however, and it was only by luck that I saw you running again. You'd changed your kit. You'd even started to wear a baseball cap, which I'm sorry to say didn't do you any favours at all.

I do think we were similar people though, you and me, like kindred spirits and by some coincidence or another we'd regularly end up at the same place. Like the time I saw you outside your office at lunchtime. You looked harassed and I wanted to check you were okay, say a few comforting words. I waved but your eyes were concealed by sunglasses, making it difficult to see if you were looking in my direction or not. I liked those glasses by the way— subtle, delicate and unlike your baseball cap, they suited you perfectly.

Then of course there was the final time I saw you. It was early evening, but warm enough for couples and groups of friends to be sitting outside one of the many cafes in town. You were on your own and looked as though you were waiting to meet someone. I tried to say hello, be friendly and to tell you there were no hard feelings about what you'd done. I know the court told me I wasn't allowed to go anywhere near you but I thought you wouldn't mind this once.

You looked beautiful, in that natural, special way of yours—so different from those women who try too hard. Your hair had been released from its ponytail and was resting on your shoulders, where it blended perfectly with the top of your blue cotton dress. There was a hint of make-up to accentuate rather than suffocate your gentle features. You looked like the girl next door I'd always dreamt of knowing. You looked amazing.

'Hiya!' I shouted. 'Suzie, it's me!'

That's all I said. How could that be so wrong? I thought it would make you smile to see me again. I thought you might want to have a chat, realise your mistake and how wrong you were about me.

Instead, you looked back in the way only a woman can. Not in a pitiful way, not hateful, but with disgust. It was only a swift glance in my direction before you looked to the ground, your previous soft features hardening into revulsion at the thought that a man like me would dare to try and make contact with you again. You turned your back, walked away and around the nearest corner. It was my turn to be angry and shocked this time. For a moment I kept looking forward at the space you'd recently vacated, unable to move but then I did.

I used to be something. I used to be something you know and I wanted to tell you how rude you'd been to me over the last few months. Just because I'd taken your picture a few times and happened to be in the same place as you on several occasions.

I'd left flowers on your doorstep every day for two months and how did you repay me? By going to the police, then making threats, then making me stand in front of a judge. Just because you were young and beautiful didn't give you the right to reject me the way you did that night or any other night, so I followed you. I wanted to let you know once and for all that you were out of order and that I was bored of both your teasing and your games.

You knew I was behind you. The thud of my boots tracing your steps, the click of your heels increasing in pace the closer I came. You flicked your head to one side and paused, turned, beckoned me towards you. I hesitated too and kept my distance. I could tell it was the last thing you expected. Then you took off your heels, put them in your hand and started to run.

I kept following, gaining with every step until we came to a road. You should have stopped, looked, listened—

paid attention to the code we were taught at school, but instead you kept running. There was a screech of brakes, then silence as though time itself was holding its breath, then a thud, then a scream.

By the time I reached you, your crumpled body was lying on the rocks in the stream I can hear from my bench in the park if the wind blows in a certain direction. Your blue cotton dress clung to you and a cloud of blood surrounded you, then started to drift with the flow of the water. Blue and red, red and blue, like the colours of the kingfisher I see all too rarely but just like you, its grace and sophistication seduces me back to the park day after day.

I nearly went. I nearly went straight away to the police station to confess but decided not to. I would've told them I was only trying to reassure you, that I hadn't meant to frighten you and you simply had the wrong idea about me from the start.

But if I'd gone they'd only have sent me away. They might even have charged me with wasting police time. Following someone down the street doesn't constitute a crime, even if a restraining order is in place, not without the victim reporting the crime and of course you now cannot do this.

I won't write again. This is the last letter I'll write and at least this time I know you definitely won't reply. I just wanted to let you know I forgive you for what you did, after all that's what friends do isn't it, forgive? I've found someone else too but this time it'll be different. I won't crowd her like I did with you and instead let her live, let her breathe, let her fly like a bird. If anything, this time I'll let her come to me.

I won't forget you though; you don't have to worry about that. As well as having your picture in my wallet, every time I see a kingfisher, every fleeting glimpse, every flash of blue and red, I'll of course be reminded of you.

# The Missus – Sue Thomas

It was difficult to understand when Joe went away and I was left with 'the missus'. I know that was her name because Joe and I used to have morning chats on our walks. Joe would say, 'Come on, boy, let's get out from under the missus' feet,' or when we got home, 'Come on let's wipe your feet or the missus will skin us alive.'

I was with Joe since I was a puppy, and we had a great understanding. Joe did everything for me. The missus sometimes used to say, 'Come on, Joe, he's your dog; get him fed and out for a walk, I need to do some shopping.'

One morning, really early, the missus locked me out in the garden; there were flashing lights and a loud noise, men running into the house. Then they took Joe away, and the missus went with them. I was outside for hours and it was raining. I tried hiding under a bush, but I started shivering and was really hungry. Joe hadn't given me my breakfast or taken me for my usual walk.

It was very dark when the missus got back and I waited patiently outside the back door, my tail wagging although I didn't really feel happy, just very relieved. Suddenly I realised the light had come on in the bedroom. I could see the missus moving about. I felt very sad and forgotten, curling my body round so that my nose touched my tail, I lay on the doorstep waiting…

Then, what seemed like hours later suddenly all the lights came on and I heard the missus quickly coming down the stairs. She opened the back door and picked me up in a big soft warm towel. 'Tsk tsk, you poor boy,' she said, 'I nearly forgot all about you.' She knelt down on the carpet in the lounge so we were nose to nose, rubbing and rubbing me dry, warming me up as she stroked and rubbed. 'Sorry, boy, Joe's passed on,' she whispered. 'It's just you and me now.' A large tear sliding down her cheek and landing on my nose. I licked her salty cheek as she gathered me up. I wasn't sure what she meant, but I just knew I wouldn't see Joe again. I was really surprised when the missus put me on the bed; I had never been allowed on before. Then she slid under the covers, her arm pulling me into the warmth of her body and we both instantly fell asleep.

Oh dear, I thought when I woke in the morning disorientated, I'm in trouble now. But no, the missus patted me on the head and got up to get our breakfast.

It was very quiet in the house; I missed Joe's loud voice, but knew the missus missed it more, so I never complained. I missed my daily walks too, but I wasn't as young as I used to be, so made the most of being let out in the garden. Joe and the missus had a daughter, Sue, who came twice or sometimes three times a week and she would take me to the park with her children. I enjoyed that, except it was sad not being with Joe.

Time passed and everyone got more cheerful, except sometimes the missus would forget to feed me, and other times she would feed me twice a day. When Sue arrived she would call, 'Have you fed the dog, Mum?'

And the missus would say, 'Of course I have'.

I would try to look appealingly at Sue, sitting in front of her and wagging my tail desperately but she would say, 'Now, now don't be greedy.' Eventually she would say it with real concern and start checking the food levels. And thank goodness she caught on and started feeding me on her visits.

One day there was a big upheaval and men came and started taking the furniture out of the house. Sue sat me on her lap and said, 'I'm really sorry, boy, but Mum needs to go into a care home and I am not able to keep you; don't be sad I'm sure we will find you a good home, though not many would take on an old boy like you.' I didn't really understand but she cried a lot when she put me in her car. 'Come on, boy,' she said, 'let's go and see Mum before we take you to the kennels.' I'm not sure why, but my heart lurched and I felt very sad.

At the care home there were a lot of people. Ladies like the missus. Men like Joe, some sad, some cheerful. They all crowded round me and the missus and before long they were all smiling and cheerful as I wagged my tail feeling really happy for the first time for a long while. Then Sue said, 'Come on, boy, we have to go.'

I slumped to the ground and felt like crying myself.

A tall younger lady said, 'Wait a minute, can we have a chat in my office?' I crept up to the missus and took comfort from her lifting me into her lap and she stroked me, her body heaving with tears running down her cheeks. I licked them dry and thought back to another day...

All of a sudden Sue came rushing out of the office saying, 'I don't believe this, Mum, matron says Boy can stay, he can stay!! She saw the reaction our Boy created in you and the residents and now Boy is the resident care dog!! He cheered you all up, he can stay...'

I love my new life and all my new friends and I especially love the missus.

# The Price Of Love – Joseph Govan

David walked out of the shower room, steam pouring out of the open door. He found his suit, freshly pressed, lying on his bed, a red carnation held in the breast pocket. He dressed and walked slowly down the stairs. She was waiting for him at the door, their two children beside them. They traded chaste pleasantries at the threshold and he left with the premise of returning in a couple of hours, a brisk walk taking him out the front garden and down the street.

Theirs was a union planned in the old ways, by the logic of inter-family politics and economics, not of love. 'You don't have to love her,' David's father told his young son on the eve of his wedding day. 'All you need to do is put a baby in her and make sure that there is enough money so that she can keep the household. After that, you can do what you want. Hell! You can even fuck some young things on the side, provided you're not too blatant about it of course. Loving and caring? Nonsense! This is about duty, you have a family now and your duty is to look out for them.'

David had thought about those words a lot over the years, especially recently. The day was cold for the season and the people he met as he walked past identikit houses were all bundled up. Those who knew him nodded as he passed, a token of respect, but no one spoke a word to him. He was in his own world, not to be disturbed.

By some measures their marriage was a fruitful one. They had two beautiful children, a large and comfortable home, even a dog. All that most would envy. But his nights with her were cold. He felt no passion for her. It was all he could do to sleep with her those few scant times that gave them children. After the second child that part of the marriage dried up. They shared a bed, they shared meals, and they shared little else.

He passed homes, businesses, bare, stark offices. Many were closed, the butcher's, the greengrocer's, their proprietors elsewhere.

As a measure of escape, for them both, David took up other interests. There was a gentlemen's club in the town that his father had recommended. There he was able to socialise with other like-minded men, men who had all found something lacking in their home lives. Some days they would play games, gamble, or occasionally just sit and talk, their thoughts liberally lubricated with scotch. It was there that he felt at home, not in the house he owned.

There were a large number of cars parked outside the parish church. From inside he could hear the murmuring of an ongoing service. He came to the gate and paused, taking a moment to gather his thoughts.

After a year in the club David had developed a strong rapport with a tight group of friends. They were as close to him as family. He would share with them far more than he would with the people in his house. But amongst all of them the closest, deepest friendship had to be with Alan. His soul mate if such a thing really existed.

David passed through the door of the church and took a seat right at the back. The priest had just started and few looked back, those who did taking one look and turning away instantly. The words from the altar were droning and hard to follow. His mind drifted again.

Alan and David became almost inseparable; they would sometimes spend whole nights together, enjoying the repartee, finding each other intellectually stimulating. Until one long night, when alcohol and passion let loose and brought previously hidden feelings to the fore. It was remarkable, terrifying, so unlike everything all David's upbringing had told him to expect. But it felt right, so very right.

The priest addressed the congregation, his hand pointing to an unseen few in the front row. At his prompt the whole mass of people got to their feet. David stayed seated, his head a maelstrom.

It wasn't easy to keep things a secret, in a community as close-knit as theirs it never is. There were looks in the street, harsh words behind closed doors, but no one ever dared say anything. Everyone else has too much of their own foibles to ever risk saying anything in the open. There was only one word, in all that time, at home. They were together at the dinner table when she looked up, put down her knife and fork and said to him, 'I don't care what you do outside this house but you must remember, you have a wife, you have a family, you must care for them.'

The service continued. There were calls and responses from the pulpit then the sound of people standing again and shuffling towards the front. David, his hands on his lap, sat for a second and started to rise.

For months, years, everything was perfect. But with increased closeness, it got harder and harder for them to leave each other to return home. They would muse sometimes about leaving it all behind, starting a new life together but whenever he did so David remembered the words of his father and wife and thought better of it.

He walked slowly down the pews, taking his place in the queue as it slowly shuffled its way up towards the altar. His mind filled with trepidation.

David remembered the knocking on the door in the middle of the night. He remembered Alan there, carry-all over his shoulders, car at the kerb. He had taken their lovers' whispers to heart, he wanted to come and take David away with him. He remembered saying that he had a life, responsibilities that he could not, would not, leave. He remembered closing the door as Alan turned away into the night.

The last person in front of David turned away and there it was. The coffin, a mahogany monolith, was right in front of him. On its top, nestled in a sea of carnations, Alan's face looking through the glass of an old framed photograph. It was closed casket; monoxide can leave such a horrible colour.

David took the carnation from his breast pocket and placed it amongst the others on the coffin. He didn't turn to the family; they would neither welcome him nor acknowledge his presence. He moved on in silence.

He watched silently from the sidelines as the coffin was carried out of the church and stayed in the back as it was brought to its final resting place. He did not talk or reminisce with others, he did not follow the rest for food and the pub, he waited maybe a minute longer than the rest, then he went home.

A warm lunch was waiting for David when he passed through the door of his home. She served a generous portion onto his plate, much more than usual, and left a hand on his shoulder, just for a second, as she went to go.

It was a thank you for staying, for not taking the road that Alan had travelled, but David knew there was no fear of that.

He had looked at the price of love, of broken promises, shattered lives, and found it too high to pay.

# The Snip – Claudia Crutwell

Polly checked herself in the hallway mirror and undid the top button on her blouse before entering the study to deliver George his mug of green tea. He was rammed up close to the computer screen, bookshelves sagging around him, CD Roms stacked on the floor, wastepaper basket wedged to the brim with discarded reports. George only noticed her when she tried to place the mug amongst the debris on his desk and chose one of his running magazines.

'Not there,' he said and thrust forwards the mouse mat as an alternative.

'Are you going to be much longer with that?'

'I don't know. Another hour maybe. Why?'

'Nothing, nothing.' She took a step back. 'Nothing.'

'What?' He swivelled round in his chair to look at her. His balding pate backlit by the computer screen was like one of those golf balls that glow in the dark, designed for executives who were, like him, too busy to play by day.

Polly paused a moment to allow him to take her in: to clock the new fuchsia blouse with nails to match and the straightened hair. There was the same faint perplexity in his expression as she might expect if she served cottage pie for dinner with a breadcrumb topping, instead of the usual mashed potato.

'Nothing,' she said. 'Listen, but when are you going to get around to employing someone else to proofread these reports? It's late. You should be coming to bed.'

'I'd love to, believe me.' He made a play of eyeballing her breasts.

She glanced down and feigned surprise at the gaping buttonhole.

George turned back to the screen and scrolled down.

'Got to get this done. I'm off to Zurich tomorrow, remember? Coming back early Friday for the op.'

'I know. So that only gives us tonight to…'

'To what?'

She bit her lip. 'What I mean is you won't see me or the girls all week.'

'When do I ever see the girls? They're in bed by the time I get home most nights.' He took a sip of the green tea as if, like his children, it were a remembered duty.

Polly picked up a framed photo from the desk: George at the finish line of the London Marathon, clasping to his sodden armpits all four daughters. She rubbed at a smudge on the glass.

'Hannah started school today.'

'Oh shit.'

'It's okay.'

'No, it's not okay. I wish you'd reminded me this morning. I would have made sure I got home early in time to see her. How did it go?'

'You know Hannah. She just gets on with it, doesn't she? No tears, no having to prize her off me, finger by finger, unlike Melissa.'

'Maybe I could pop up and see if she's still awake?'

'She's not. She's exhausted.' Polly put the photo back in a more prominent position on the desk.

George stared at it.

'So,' he said. 'Hannah in full-time education. The last of the brood.'

'I know, wonderful isn't it?' Polly tossed her hair which, with the curls ironed out, the hairdresser said made her look ten years younger.

'What about you? Are you okay?' George's finger hovered over the mouse, awaiting her reassurance before clicking. 'You're not, you know, feeling too emotional about it?'

'Only if by emotional you mean bloody ecstatic. I had the whole day to myself. Drove into town, did some shopping, got my hair and nails done, lunch in Starbucks, even had time for a nap after. Six hours of freedom.'

She felt in her trouser pocket for Spot, Hannah's favourite finger puppet. He had been to Starbucks and the hairdressers too.

'At one point I had four under five, you know.'

'That's a good boast, isn't it?' George smiled, highlighted a phrase on the screen and typed in a correction.

'Not many people can say that.'

'Not many.'

'And now at last, I can be me.' She threw up her arms in the air and wiggled her hips like a runner crossing the finish line, though she'd never run a race in her life.

'Four gorgeous schoolgirls,' he laughed. 'I'm so incredibly virile.'

'Yeah, yeah. It's all down to you. Anyway, it's just as well I never craved a boy.'

'Thank God. You could go on forever like that,' George said.

'Some people do.' Polly put her hand to her empty tummy.

'Being a free woman suits you. You look nice, by the way.'

He pawed at the mouse, leaning into the screen, wading through columns of figures to get to the next section of prose.

'Can you imagine actually going back to nappies and night feeds, mushy food and projectile vomiting?' Polly rescued some sheets of paper in danger of sliding onto the floor and tapped them into shape on the desk like a newsreader winding up a story. 'Ugh!' she said. 'I couldn't stand it.'

'Uh-huh. Yeah.'

'I'm going to ring the agency tomorrow and see what openings they've got.'

'You want to go back to work?' He carried on looking at the screen but she could tell he'd momentarily lost his focus.

'I might have to update my training, but why shouldn't I?'

'No reason, I'm just a bit surprised, that's all.'

'You think I'm just going to mope around the house wanting another baby?'

He pushed back his chair from the desk and rolled his head from side to side, cricking his neck muscles, giving her space to speak.

'Hannah's at school now. You're getting the snip on Friday. Everything's changing. I need something to occupy me. I need to feel like I've got something to contribute.'

'Well of course, if that's how you feel, give the agency a call. We'll be a double-income family. Fantastic. On the other hand,' his eyes skirted the surrounding bookshelves, 'I'd have thought there was plenty for you to occupy yourself with around the house.'

'Like?'

'Like this room could do with a good tidy.'

'I'm going to ignore that.' She prodded his shoulder.

He reached out and soothed her hip with his palm.

'So, are you coming to bed now?' she said.

'Got to get this done.' He pulled his hand away. 'You go. I couldn't trust myself to keep away from you anyway. Knowing it's off limits only makes it all the more tempting. Roll on Friday, hey? I never thought I'd look forward to an operation so much.'

'You remember we used to practise the rhythm method?' She swayed her shoulders, twisting a strand of her hair.

'I do remember. And I remember Melissa. It failed.'

'Probably wouldn't fail now. We're too old to conceive.'

'Speak for yourself.'

Last weekend, when Melissa had resisted going to a birthday party because she felt too shy, Polly had finally persuaded her by agreeing she shouldn't go.

'You're right. Better play safe.' She confiscated his unfinished mug of tea. 'We'll wait till Friday, or until you've recovered from the op. However many weeks that's going to be. I imagine you'll be sore for a while. I just thought, what are the chances of anything happening tonight?…But, no, you're right. Better not risk it.'

She turned to go, sensing him weaken through a kind of physical telepathy borne of all their years together.

'Night, night. Don't forget to switch off the lights.'

She had barely reached the bedroom above when she heard the shut-down jingle on his computer. Climbing into bed naked, she placed a pillow on the floor beside her, ready to slip under her hips afterwards, once he'd dropped off to sleep. She lay back and listened to the flick of the light switches and waited for him to mount the stairs towards her.

# Unfinished Business –
# Courtney Jennings

The oak was the largest she'd ever seen, she always thought. It was beautiful and wise looking. Its branches were spindly, and its trunk twisted upward into the boughs in the most intriguing way. The bench beneath its shade was a comforting spot—one she visited often. She sat quietly, alone, staring across the well-tended, fenced-in yard. The birds' song and the hum of a calm wind were the only sounds surrounding her.

'It's peaceful, isn't it?' he said, interrupting her daydreaming. She didn't bother looking over at him. She kept her gaze on the wind-bent flowers, her thoughts on the calming rustle of the leaves above her.

'Do you know why they call this The Angel Yard, Lucy?' His voice was soft—a whisper.

A quiet sigh was the only acknowledgment she'd offer—a subtle rise in her chest and shoulders.

'Well,' he continued, looking out across the scattered, sun-whitened headstones. 'Some say they can feel a presence here, the embrace of their loved ones passed.' Her heart slowed, feeling heavier. 'Some say, they've talked to them, even seen them.'

Lucy sighed more dramatically this time, wishing that were true. 'You know I don't believe in things like that,' she said dryly. She could feel him staring at her, but wouldn't look over. She didn't have to; she knew his reaction to her disbelief all too well. 'Only the weak believe that way,' she added. 'Those who can't deal with life and its disgustingly harsh reality.'

His voice was sad sounding, a hopelessness plaguing it. 'Yet, you've seen it so many times now with your own beautiful eyes.' He reached out carefully and rested his hand softly atop hers. She flinched inwardly, not allowing him to notice, her face pinched in her desperate attempt to still her shaking hands.

She said simply, 'I see what my heart wants me to see…nothing more.'

Nowadays, her voice was a dead, monotonous sort of drone; not at all oozing with the buzzing sweetness it used to.

'Faith is for everyone, Lucy,' he reminded her. 'Even the stubborn.' He squeezed her hand tighter, as if he could convince her with just a touch. 'Some seek proof a lifetime and never find it, but *you*…proof came to you. You didn't have to search. Your proof…*is right here*.' He pulled her hand onto his lap, and his fingers stroked hers, desperate to make his point.

'You're just a figment of my own desperate desires.'

'You don't believe that.'

'I do,' Lucy argued, steadying her dead gaze on the closest leaning stone. 'The mind is a very powerful thing.'

It was quiet again, only for a moment, before he spoke softly into her ear. 'I love you, Lucy.'

He smiled sadly at her internal struggle with her faith. He'd seen that confusion deep in her eyes so many times before. He always knew he'd found Lucy for a reason. He'd been her strength, and he knew how hard it'd been for her since he'd gone.

She sucked in a composing breath, chest tight. Tears welled in her eyes, and she finally looked at him. She squeezed his fingers in hers. Her struggle hesitated, and a distinct smile of freedom and relief replaced her pain…and his too. His thumb caught a single tear at her trembling jaw, and he faded away before her eyes.